Pulp
&
Circumstance

Hardboiled Histories & Disreputable Genres

**Radical Rootless Cosmopolitan Culture-Punk
Historical Fictions**

New and collected narratives

Peter Ullian

Swamp Angel Press

DEDICATION

To my wife and kids, for everything.

To Donna Minkowitz and Lit Lit, for a place to dream.

To Stanza Books, for the books and inspiration.

The Critics on the Work of Peter Ullian:

"A cross between David Mamet and the Marx Brothers . . . provocative and witty, arresting . . . an abundance of inventive wit . . . a flair for language . . . his own brand of desperate comedy . . . a real talent . . . Ullian has a distinctive voice" (***The Cleveland Plain Dealer***)

"Singularly satisfying, winning, heart rending, punchy, button-pushing, irresistible . . imaginatively rendered . . . palpably energizing" (***The New York Times***)

"Taut, absorbing . . . great style and crisp wit" (***Variety***)

"Pulsing, power-packed, vital and visionary" (***Out in Denver***)

"An intriguing blend of the macabre and the humorous . . . romance, intrigue, humor, violence" (***The Beacon Journal***)

"Quirky, crackling" (***The Village Voice***)

"Highly entertaining . . .wryly satirical" (***BBC Merseyside***)

"Nearly perfect . . . very accomplished" (***Chicago Theater Beat***)

"Wildly imaginative" (***The Press Enterprise***)

"Wonderfully funny and . . . filled with invention" (***The Hollywood Reporter***).

Table of Contents

Four: Once Upon a Time in a Fading Empire

Five: Once Upon a Time to Come

ACKNOWLEDGMENTS

Stories included in this collection have appeared in *Frontier Tales Magazine* and *Crimeucopia: Say What Now?*

One: Once Upon a Time South of 14th Street

Hester Street Hideaway: A Lower East Side Love Story

a historical fiction of Prohibition

Originally commissioned by En Garde Arts and performed as a monologue play as part of their theatrical production, *A Secret History of the Lower East Side*, September 1998. Anne Hamburger, Producer and Artistic Director.

Hester Street Hideaway, Part One

Hester Street: and I wasn't moving much anymore. Everything else moved here, but not me. The pushcart vendor calls would ring out, and shatter my sleep, but I wouldn't move; not much point in moving those days in Jew Town, with the wind whipping across the East River and ripping me to icy shreds, with the thunder going *ba-boom* above my head, and the lightening snap-cracking above the girders of the Williamsburg Bridge; so, I stayed in my rickety bed in a crumbling room in a decaying tenement on Hester Street.

I looked at her left-overs--a hairbrush, strands of her Irish-red hair between the teeth; a pair of flowered knickers, tossed in the corner; her Goddamn *goyische* rosary hung on a doorknob, where she left it when she left me.

Why do Jewish boys always fall hardest for the Catholic girls?

"How in hell can I love ye when ye won't leave me alone?" she said to me the night before she walked out the door of our Hester Street hideaway, her Irish lilt decayed into an Irish slur from too much Irish whiskey. "Sure, but love for ye is like a life sentence on Blackwell's Island, and when I stare into the looking glass, do I not see the thick barbed wire wrapped around me head?" And so, she left me with her crown of thorns but left me her rosary -- what am I supposed to do with a rosary? -- and I stopped moving, until the day I went to the Essex Street Market.

As my friend Manny Gold used to say, "da Essex Street Market is da Essex Street Market is da Essex Street Market," and I had no idea just what the hell he meant by that. But I went to the Essex Street Market that afternoon, because even when there's nothing left to get up for, sometimes your body just takes you places, and you might as well not complain, because you can probably use the exercise.

And I also wanted to pick up the Lincoln.

In the market, I looked around at the chicken gizzards and fish heads, with their glazed eyes staring me down until I could see their slaughter as plainly as I could see my poor friend Manny Gold's recent demise. I stopped by a vendor and found myself facing the slimy corpse of an octopus, its tentacles wrapped around its body like it had smothered itself in its own salty death-grip. I asked the man how much and he told me $1.25, and I told him, "$1.25 for that bulbous ball of sea jelly?" and he told me that octopus is a delicacy in Japan. He was a Greek, this vendor, with a crooked nose and sunken eyes, probably a member of the Congregation Jania on Broome Street, and I asked him how he knew this about the octopus, being a Greek, a Sephardim, and clearly not Japanese, but he did not have an answer for me, and proceeded to try to convince me that, under certain conditions, octopus is kosher.

Manny Gold was my friend, you see, even though he was crazy as a loon. I'll give you a ferinstance: Once upon a time we'd been dispatched to collect a debt from this welscher on Rivington. Manny stripped the poor slob naked and dressed him with an octopus that he'd bought from this same Greek

at the Essex Street Market – which only cost us fifty cents -
- and which he draped around the welsher's waist like a
loin cloth. After several hours, the octopus had dried
around the man's testicles tight as wet leather sitting in the
sun, and it took us an hour and a half to pry it loose, after
which the guy's balls were tiny as grapes, and he threw up
for hours. And then he crawled to a corner, lifted up the
floorboards, pulled out a wad of C-notes, and made good on
his debt.

Manny went home that night and laughed and laughed
when he told this story to his wife, a long-suffering, patient
woman from Odessa who had finally reached the limits of
her suffering and patience, and she told Manny what a fool
he was, and what a terrible man he was to boot. And when
she'd finished telling him all this, Manny looked her in the
eyes and told her in a voice as sincere as Jack Dempsey's
left hook, "What? Did I ever claim to be a *mensch*, dolly? I
never said I was a moral man, not me. I only said I was a
serious one."

So, I left the octopus vendor, and I picked up the
Lincoln, which was parked on the street under a tarpaulin,
and I drove over the Williamsburg Bridge and into
Brooklyn.

Manny Gold's only useful skill was an incredible facility
with automobiles. If there was any poetry in his life, it was
his relationship with internal-combustion engine-propelled
metal machines. He called himself the "Jalopy Jew," part
shtarker and part steel, as he liked to say, and when he
drove his car with the accelerator pressed to the floor, he
became a great big mesh of flesh and metal and blood and
motor oil and muscle and chrome. And, he said, that's
exactly how he hoped to die, in a great big, charred glob of
those six elements on some far away American byway far
from the choking city early one Sunday morning, as the

goyische world went to church, and his soul flew to heaven or to hell or to parts unknown.

But Manny, poor Manny, he didn't get to die that way.

Manny once told me "Never look back when ya' drive, pally. Always stare straight ahead, dat's what I do, yesiree. Drive by intuition, yesiree. By pure instinct. Ease inta da next lane, pally. Don't reduce speed. Take corners as fast as possible, trust me on dis, pally. Never stop. Oh, and one more thing, and if you remember anything I just told ya', remember dis -- always drive like dere's a person tied to a rope at da back a' your car. Drive like ya' knew who it was at the end of dat rope."

Well, as it turned out, Manny was the person at the end of that rope, and that's how Manny died, with a rope tied around his neck, bouncing and scraping along behind a Lincoln V-8 on the black tar of the humming, rumbling Williamsburg Bridge.

And as I hurried over the bridge, the steel cables whizzing past me, I knew that he was right, for, contrary to his instructions, I sneaked a look back towards Manhattan, and I swear I could see Manny's ghost, the rope around his neck connecting him to the Lincoln like a lethal umbilical cord, as he went a-bouncing and a-dragging along behind me.

This is why Manny died: we had stolen $60,000 from our employee, Meyer Lansky. Bennie Siegel, Meyer's partner, found Manny drinking in our favorite spot down on Bowery and tied Manny to the back of his car, and dragged him over the bridge by his neck until poor Manny was thoroughly, extremely, and completely dead.

It was that same night that my Wild Irish Rose and I locked ourselves into our room on Hester Street, waiting to see if Bennie Siegel would find us, too. We stayed there for days, cocooned in our crumbling room, the shades drawn, making love by the glow of streetlamps, knowing every night could be our last. And then I woke up one morning to find her gone.

That was when I went to Essex Street to get my Lincoln V-8.

I loved my Lincoln V-8. It was a big old thing, with lots of room to stash and conceal things . . . like sixty thousand dollars . . . and a top speed of -- can you believe it? -- 80 miles per hour. I drove the car. Manny fixed it. That's what we did in the Meyer and Bugs gang. Those days, they were heady days. Prohibition was still in effect, and there was money to be made for people with the stones to make it. Lansky understood that. He ran his operation on the principles of American entrepreneurship, the same principles that made millionaires out of men with names like Ford, Carnegie, Rockefeller, Morgan. As Lansky liked to say, "one day, we'll be bigger than U.S. Steel."

Lansky liked me because I wore glasses, and I liked to read books. I was an egghead, like him. That's why they called me the "Professor." Now, let me just say, reading as much as I did, you might think I was something special, but reading, for a poor kid in Jewtown, wasn't so hard to come by, with all the libraries and settlement houses and educational alliances set up by wealthy German Jews for the purposes of teaching us uncouth Litvak greenhorns how to be more *American*. Anyway, all this reading allowed me to use impressive words, like, say, *debauchery*, and, just in case you don't believe me, I intend to use just that word in an actual sentence in the not-too-distant future. So, I ask you to think of me not as a fella trying to speak above his station, but, instead, as a linguistic victim of good intentions.

But anyway, I am reminded at this point about what my girl said to me our last night alone in the dark of our single-room Hester Street hideaway, which was this:

"Sure, but I knew I was in a fecking heap o' trouble when the fecking freaks at the fecking Dime Museum on Coney Island started to make me blubber like a fecking infant, they did. I was crying all the time, I was. Sure, but was I not reduced to a shriveled ball of emotional wreckage? Did I not fall for every trick? Did not every naked, manipulative string they pulled send me into hysterical fits of violent sobbing? Did I not return time and time again to the Dime Museum, in the hope of exorcising me fecking state of emotional instability? Aye, the bearded woman, I knew in me heart, was running from the pain of a broken romance, rejected by her lover's disinclination towards facial hair, and did this knowledge not cause me to pour forth a bitter torrent of tears, and would I not rush out into the sunlight and collapse on the boardwalk? Like some kind of a fecking invalid, I was. Would I not develop ulcerous pangs of empathy for the Wild Man, that hairy beast, plucked from his home in the jungles of darkest Peru, and forced to prance in chains before the mob o' fecking thrill-seeking pagans standing there before him? Did I not become positively suicidal at the plight of the Siamese Twins, never to know a moment's peace or solitude from each other, sharing every damn 'ting from taking a shite to the pangs o' love that ached inside their one, shared heart? Sure, but I knew what was happening to me. Sure, but I knew I was falling victim to the cheapest sort of low-brow sentiment. Aye, but could I fecking help meself? That I could not. Sure, but they had me where they wanted me. Just like you have me where you want me. That is what you've done to me. I won't let you do it anymore. Ye fecking gob a' shite, ye."

I was thinking about her saying this, and so I drove out to Coney Island, but her Dime Museum was closed, boarded up. I stood on the boardwalk and looked at the seagulls flying above the surf. Then I drove back to my neighborhood, the Lower East Side, where I was raised, where I worked, and where I expected, very soon, to die.

And as the sun set, I decided to visit my family, for one

last time.

This Town

The Lower East Side. Jewtown. This part of town was always like a beetle on its back. Down by the river's edge, kids played in the left-overs of the factories and the warehouses, swimming naked with the East River rats, and when it rained little pieces of abandoned buildings washed into the water.

A big black cloud drifted across the sky. A telephone pole was framed against the hazy light, and it looked like the big crucifix at the end of her rosary, outlined against the tired bloodshot sun which was sinking in the air behind like it just didn't give a good Goddamn anymore. I had a thick layer of grime on my shoes, and I could smell the stagnant East River water. I stopped off at the old Saloon on Bowery for a quick one to brace myself before going home.

Ah, the Bowery. I'd spent too much time in this part of town, where members of all ethnicities met in debasement and . . . *debauchery* . . . trying to drink enough to keep from going crazy until they could just pass out. I should have left right then, put this dirty old Manhattan Island behind me once and for all, but something was calling me. Calling me back to this dirty old town. Back to the broken bottles on the dirty old street. Back to the vigilante gangs of poor angry young men patrolling the dirty edges of their ethnic enclaves. Back to the sad old cantors cantoring their sad old Kaddish through the windows of their sad old crumbling shuls. Back to the warehouses filled with trucks of bootleg beer. Back to the pushcart venders calling their wares. Back to the whores on Allen Street. Back to a dirty old bed with creaking old bed boards and squeaking old bed springs and dirty little bed-bugs to share it with. Something was calling me. There was nothing to find, nothing to return to. No happy memories to dredge up. No childhood haunts to return to. Just these lonesome, filthy, old, crowded streets and the big black sky peeking over the tenement roofs and the dirt on my shoes, and the dust in the air, and the smell of cheap tobacco and herring and the taste of stale beer.

So, I went home. Sweet. Home. Fifth floor tenement walk-up. Railroad apartment. Two rooms. Two windows. One looking out on the street. The other at the airshaft. Bathtub in the kitchen. Public toilet down the hall. Dinner for the entire family, day in and day out, consisted of the following: A loaf of pumpernickel bread for a dime. Two herrings at a penny each. Three pounds of potatoes for another penny. On Fridays: meat soup made from bologna ends and bones and leftovers from the butcher, three pounds worth at six cents a pound. Home. Sweet. Home.

First thing I did was to say hello to my little brother. My younger brother, I should tell you, was a man of a thousand attitudes, most of them bad, a man of a thousand moods, nine hundred ninety-nine of them foul, and the law of averages being what it is, he was in one of the nine-hundred ninety-nine when I found him, sitting in the bathtub in the kitchen, and he looked at me like he didn't know who I was, and this is what he said to me:

"I live here, ok, ya' see? I live here in the tub. I haven't left it for three years, ok, ya' see? It's the cat's whiskers, it's the bee's knees. 'Cept the water's gettin' cold. The water's gettin' colder than . . . some really cold water, I don't mind tellin' ya'.

"Every morning, ok, I wake up at six thirty when my *mamme* comes in to make my *tatteh* breakfast, ya' see? And I sit in the tub here, and I listen to my *tatteh* while he eats the breakfast in the next room, ok? And he slurps and chomps and smacks, and they talk, my *mamme* and *tatteh*, but they're so tired that they don't even hear each other no more, ya see, just noises going yap yap yap, ok? Oh, but I hear them, ya see? Just enough so's I can't get back to sleep. And I wonder if they're talkin' 'bout me and how come I don't get outta the tub and get a mother-lovin' job. But that's a dumb thing to be wonderin', 'cause they've given up talkin' 'bout me a long time ago, ya' see? And so's I just look through the doorway into the other room and I watch my *foter* go out the door and down the stairs, to his filthy little spirit-killing seven-days-a-week job in the sweatshop -- "if you don't come in on Saturday, don't bother coming in on Sunday!" -- and sometimes I wave, but he never sees me, and he never waves back, ok? So, then I lie back in the bath, and I can't get back to sleep, but I don't get out of the tub all day, ya' see? 'Cause, holey-moley, I gotta place in the scheme of things, ok? I mean, jeepers-creepers, if I got out of this bath, trains would run off their tracks, ya see? Birds would fly upside down. Turtles would zip around at the speed of bullets. Rabbits would crawl on their bellies in slow motion. Apples would break off trees and go shooting towards the sun, ok? So, ya see, it's important that I stay right here."

I looked my younger brother in the eyes. I didn't see any sign of recognition there. I told him, "I'm your *broder.*"

And he told me, "I know that, ok? Who cares?"

I left my little brother wallowing in his bathwater and looked out the one little window in the kitchen, the one that looks out at the airshaft and the window of the building across the narrow way.

It was through this little window and this little airless airshaft that I first met *her.*

The only Irish girl on the block.

Outside in the street we never spoke, but over the years through that window, that little square opening of brick and mortar, we discovered love. As kids, we looked out on one

another as we bathed in our big iron tubs in our respective
kitchens. If we stood, we could see right across the airshaft
and into each other's apartment, kitchen, bath, invading
each other's privacy in a city too crammed to offer any. We
carried on this way for years, our own peculiar courtship,
unseen by the grown-up world behind the ragged curtain
strung across a broom handle in the doorway that
separated the kitchen from the rest of the apartment during
the weekly bath-time. Secretly tasting the forbidden each of
us was to the other. We continued our ritual through our
teenage years. Our bodies transformed: breasts and
musculature. The hair on her head as bright red as the hair
between her thighs. When our hormones kicked in, we
shared long, serious looks, as our hands and our bodies
discovered new sensations in this New World. I remember
standing on my toes, time and time again over the years,
pressed against the window, my arms and fingers stretched
to their limits, reaching towards her across the void of the
airshaft, through the dank air and the pigeon feathers and
the pigeon droppings, the odor of garbage filling my nose --
to this day I am still aroused by the smell of garbage --
trying to make contact with her as she reached back
towards me.

I achieved my first orgasm the moment our damp
fingertips finally touched. I knew I had reached maturity
both because of the attainment of my sexual response and
the increased reach of my limbs.

But I found it hard to enjoy this reverie properly with my
brother splashing away behind me, so I went into the other
room and started towards the door. But I caught a glimpse
of my *mamme* sitting in the corner, and something told me I
should say hello to her before I walked out that door
forever.

My *muter* sat there in her rocking chair, quiet as a

mouse, stitching ribbons. Her eyes were going. I could see the varicose veins in her legs, and I could see her hands gnarled with arthritis, and still she stitched, something she had done since we arrived in this dirty, squalid town, stitching ribbons together, late into the night by candlelight, selling them to the clothing stores for three cents a ribbon. And when I asked how she was and how *tatteh* was she said, "Such a life I've had to suffer. Your *foter*'s never been good to me. Your *foter*'s an old coot, and he farts when he sleeps. Such a life, I did not deserve."

So, I left my *mamme* and started towards the door again, but then I saw my *tatteh* across the room, and something told me I should say hello to him one last time before I walked out that door forever.

When I was a tot, a mere child, no more than knee-high to a grasshopper, when a stalk of grass was as high as the Woolworth building to me, my *foter* would tell me a story, which he repeated now as I watched him sharpen a rusty orange razor on a leather strap, and it went like this:

"When I was your age, son, when I was a tot, a mere child, no more than knee-high to a grasshopper, when a stalk of grass was as high as the Woolworth building to me, I was fishing down by the lake, this was in the old country you know, the old country, hard it was, very hard indeed, and pogroms, you know, the Cossacks rampaging through the *shtetel*, burning our homes, outraging our daughters and our wives, I have news for you, little man," he said, putting the rusty razor to my neck, "you are not my son. You are the bastard off-spring of your mother and her Cossack despoiler . . . but where was I? Oh yes, my story . . . . I was fishing by the lake and I caught the most beautiful trout you ever did see, gold it was, as gold as your *mutter*'s wedding ring, and as I stared at this marvel of *Hashem* and nature, the trout spoke to me, in an odd accent, because

Yiddish is not the native language of trout, their native language being something closer to Lithuanian, and the trout said to me, 'If you do not eat me, young fisherman, which I do not recommend at all because I am solid gold and I might break your teeth, I shall grant you a wish upon my return to the water.' And I thought to myself, well, I would like a mountain of gold, but how should I get such a mountain of gold back home? So, I said to the golden trout, 'Mr. Trout, I would certainly appreciate a wheel-barrow full of gold," and the trout said, 'It is done,' and I threw that golden trout back into the water of the lake, and no sooner had I done that than a wheel-barrow full of gold appeared in the middle of the lake, and promptly plopped into the water and sank two miles to the bottom. And as I watched the rings spread on the surface of the water, I heard that golden trout swimming away, gurgling and laughing like a *meshugener*. And that was when I resolved to come to America, where I had been told the streets were paved with gold.

"Such a disappointment, I had, years later, when I finally stepped off the boat."

As my *foter* repeated this story to me, I was reminded of one night when I was young, a mere child, knee-high to a grass hopper, etcetera, etcetera, and I woke up to find my *tatteh* standing in the doorway of our home -- this was in the old country, before we came to America -- where I slept next to the stove in the kitchen by my younger *brudder*, and my father was breathing heavily and with great difficulty, and he was splattered with blood from head to toe, and he said to me "I stabbed him. I stabbed him again and again and again, and he kept coming towards me, and I filled him full of holes, and he just would not die."

I went outside into the cool air of that dark night, the dead leaves rustling in the wind and the black clouds racing by the silvery moon. I looked down on the ground and found a large man in a Cossack's garb lying face down, his blood seeping from the ragged holes in his body and into the damp earth, and I looked at my *foter* breathing hard and shaking in the doorway of our small home, repeating over and over, "He just would not die, he just would not die."

"Well, *tatteh*," I said, scratching my nose and staring at the moon, "he's dead now, that's for sure."

We buried the Cossack behind the outhouse that night and never spoke of the incident again.

I noticed, the next Spring as we prepared to leave our home and emigrate to America, as I stood over the Cossack's un-marked resting place behind the outhouse, how green and rich the grass there was.

Now, all these years later, I brought up the incident for the first time, and I said: "*Tatteh*. That man we buried behind the out-house . . . was he my *foter*?"

But *tatteh* said nothing and did not look me in the eye.

I left them, stepping outside that little tenement for what I knew would be the last time, and I was about to get back into the Lincoln, when it struck me that I couldn't leave until I had located my sister.

I found her later that night. My little *shvester*. The only one of us siblings born in America. I remembered her as a child with her jet-black hair in pigtails. Her hair was still jet-black, but no longer in pigtails, and now she was walking the street on Allen, selling herself as her wares, her belly swollen in the eighth month of pregnancy.

"Oh, he was a handsome man, alright, the little schemer" she told me, staring at her feet. "He had shiny black hair, and a nose as sharp as a knife. He was prince charming, he was, the *schmuckie* little bastard. He was an educated man, a traveling man, and he'd been to school, alright, fat lot of good it did me, educated seed'll get you just as knocked up as any other kind. He said he loved me, ooboy, wish I knew then how cheaply that sentiment goes for, now that I think of all the men who loved me for the price of a meal. We went to dances, and when we made love that night in the shadows of a doorway, our skin lit by the glow of the gas lamp and the moon, somehow, I knew that he wasn't gonna be around the next morning. And, sure enough, he was gone. And I ain't expectin' him to be back either, not any time soon."

At this point, I'd made all my stops, but I decided to make one more before embarking on my journey, so, I went to the Bowery for a drink.
Then I had another.
This was followed by a third.
I maintained this pace through the night.
I lost count sometime around dawn.

Hester Street Hideaway, Part Two

Honestly, the Bowery at six in the morning when you've been drinking all night is a gut-wrenching sight that twists the beer-fueled knot in your stomach into a high-tension cable wrapped around a steel girder that used to be your intestines. This piss-dark dawn has thorns that pierce your eyeballs and send a stiletto through your skull and into the middle of your brain, where it carves out its initials in your nervous system until you put an end to your throbbing misery and shoot yourself dead like a wounded horse, or pass out, whichever comes first, and whichever comes easier.

And, as I sat there in my Lincoln V-8 driving through the narrow streets, I seriously considered putting my revolver to my own head, considered it so seriously that I could feel my thumb pull back the hammer and my finger slowly squeeze the trigger.

But then I saw my friend, Manny Gold, sitting next to me on the passenger seat, his face all scraped and bloody, the rope burn deep and fresh around his throat like a raw, fleshy necklace, a broken-toothed grin plastered on his twisted face. He spoke, or tried to, his lips gibbering and quivering, but he made no sound, just drooled a thin stream of gooey pink saliva, which seemed to have no end, until I put the pistol to his temple and splattered his brains across the interior of the automobile.

My head jerked up from my chest then, and I found myself facing the oncoming headlights of a very large truck coming in my direction down a very narrow street.

I realized I'd drifted to the wrong side of the street. I swerved quickly. The truck's horns blared at me, and I spun out, crashing into the side of the Bank of the United States, the glass on one side of the car shattering and showering the interior. The Lincoln bounced off the wall, swung me into a 380° turn, and wobbled dangerously, veering towards a horse-drawn ragman's cart. But I straightened her, got her pointing in the right direction, and kept driving, as the panic-stricken horse reared and strained against its bit.

The image of Manny Gold's brains blowing out his head kept returning to my brain, which inspired me to pull over at Ratner's where I ate herring, latkes, blintzes, and red, red, red borscht.

Then I was ready to go. I got back in the Lincoln. I started driving.

But I found myself stopping back at my Hester Street Hideaway.

And there she was.

Lying naked on the bed.

Her nose gently sprinkled with freckles.

Her rosary resting between her breasts.

"I came back for this, I did," she said, fingering the black beads around her neck. "Sure, but didn't I walk into your closet, and smell your shirts? They smelled like stale sweat, they did.

"Sure, but I met a fella at the Saloon on Bowery, that little bucket of blood where we used to go a'courtin'," she said. "His name is Ed White, 'tis, and he's an old, old fella. And didn't he tell me he had a sweetheart who was half Cherokee, and was from Cherokee, Alabama? And five minutes later, did he not tell me he had a sweetheart who was half Sioux, and was from Sioux City, Iowa? And ten minutes after that, fer the life a' me, did he not turn around and tell me he had a girlfriend who was half Cuyahoga, and was from Cuyahoga County, Ohio? And, *bejasus*, did he not go on like this for hours, jumpin' all over the country and naming all these different tribes, until finally I asked him, I did, what he did for a living, and did he not tell me he drank for a living? And I told him, I did, that I thought he drank a wee bit too much, and ye know what the fecking old sod said to me? He leaned over, he did, and he smiled with broken, brown teeth, and he said 'Drinkin's not a bad habit, y'see, 'cause sometimes ye can talk to God, and sometimes He talks back.' And wouldn't ye know it, but he musta been having a conversation with God just then, 'cause he shut his eyes and started cursing up a firestorm and tried to punch the air and almost punched the side of me head. So, then I left, I did. And 'twas then that I thought to meself that in another forty years, ye'd be just like Ed White, yeself. 'Cept I don't 'spect ye to make it fer another forty years. So's I jes' came back to say goodbye and farewell to ye' one more time. Ye fecking gob a' shite, ye."

I got down on the mattress next to her then, and I kissed her sweet, red mouth, but she did not kiss me back. It was like I wasn't even there. And it occurred to me that perhaps I wasn't. Perhaps, with Bennie Siegel gunning for me, I was already a dead man, already fading from this world.

Perhaps she was kissed by a ghost.

So, now it was done. Now it was over. There was nothing left behind tying me down.

And as I drove like hell away from Hester Street and away from her, the sky turned green, and the thunder clapped over the bridge. And as I sped away from Jew Town forever, with $60,000 worth of Meyer Lansky's cash in my back seat, knowing that no matter how far I went, Bennie Siegel would never be far behind, knowing I was already a ghost, a ghost that had merely neglected to go through with the formality of leaving his body, in my rear-view mirror I watched the sun set slowly on the Lower East Side.

Like it just didn't give a good Goddamn anymore.

The End

Two: Once Upon a Time in the Pueblo of Los Angeles

Dreaming of *Pesach* with the Last Bandito

an Emile Harris story

a historical fiction of the American Frontier

Originally published in *Frontier Tales Magazine*, April 2021. Duke Pennell, Publisher and Managing Editor. Kimberly Pennell, Associate Editor.

Historical note: Emil Harris was a real person, one of the first policemen in frontier Los Angeles in the 1870s, and the only Jew on the force at that time. Some events depicted in this story really happened. Others could have. Some are purely imaginative. In all three cases, creative liberties have been taken.

For the purposes of fiction, the spelling of his first name has been changed from "Emil" to "Emile," and his real-life partner George Gard's last name to "Garde," in order to indicate a flexible fidelity to the facts.

We were in the hallway on the third floor outside the recently opened grand hotel *Casa de Pico*, the first of its kind in the pueblo of Los Angeles. We were standing on either side of the door to Room 31, behind which, we had reason to believe, we would find the bandit Three-Fingered Jack Dunleavy, possibly in the arms of one of our rare Los Angeles beauties.

I stood to the right of the door, my Henry repeater rifle in my hand. My partner, George Garde, stood to the left, holding a Whitney twelve-gage. We both stood in the hallway in our stockinged feet, having left our boots in the lobby to minimize the possibility that the sound of our footfalls would alert our three-fingered quarry to our presence.

I pantomimed my instruction that we drop low, as Three-Fingered Jack was known to make often reckless use of a pepperbox pistol, which could often prove quite deadly, not to say wildly painful.

We crouched on either side of the door, and I counted silently on my fingers . . . one . . . two . . .

Before I got to three, the door exploded and pellets flew across the hall and above our heads and embedded themselves in the painting that hung across the hall, which depicted a vista of Los Angeles from 1859 from the vantage of Fort Hill, overlooking the pueblo that at that time contained just over four thousand people.

Now, in 1874, the city was much bigger -- we had recently reached six thousand residents, according to local officials.

I peeked through the hole in the jagged wood of the door, and I could see Jack sitting on his bed in his long johns, trying to reload his pepperbox. He was indeed accompanied by a rare Angeleno beauty who sat beside him, regarding him with poorly concealed amusement, and wearing considerably less than long-johns, clothed, as she was, in only her natural splendor; I recognized her at once as Sadie "Angel Eyes" Margolis.

I kicked open the door, dived into the room in a rolling somersault, and came up at the foot of the bed, with my Henry pointed inches from Jack's face.

"Damnit!" Three-Fingered Jack cried. "Damnit all to hell and tarnation! This ain't fair! This ain't fair at all! You didn't give me no kind of a chance whatsoever!"

"Jack, I'm not supposed to give you a chance, I'm supposed to take you into custody," I said, quite reasonably, I thought.

Muttering about how poorly life had treated him, Jack continued to clumsily attempt to reload his pepperbox, an outdated and cumbersome weapon, but the favorite of this notorious bandit, road agent, horse thief, and train robber.

I jacked the lever on my Henry, hoping that most fearsome and intimidating sound would assist in bringing Jack into a more subdued state of compliance.

"Jack," I said. "I have the drop on you. Please put up your hands so I am not forced to shoot you in the face."

That seemed to take some of the wind out of his sails. Jack raised his hands and looked at me with all the bravado of a beaten dog.

He was an unhandsome man, with broken teeth, a crooked nose, and the kind of beard that looked as if it had never quite fully grown in, although he was easily in his late thirties by this time. He looked at me with such pathetic eyes that I felt sorry for him and somewhat kindly disposed. He had piled up an impressive record of robbing stagecoaches in Los Angeles County, which made him primarily Sheriff Rowland's problem, but since he was now hiding out in the City of Los Angeles proper, that made him ours.

"He's got another gun under the sheets, Detective Harris," Sadie said to me in Yiddish, as she pulled a Colt Dragoon from under the covers and handed it to me.

"Don't give him my pistol, you damned silly woman," Jack said.

I gently took the pistol from her. The Colt Dragoon is a cumbersome, heavy weapon, but it packs a wallop when used either as a firearm or a club.

"I'd have shot you when you came through that door, but this damnable pepperbox keeps discharging all its six barrels at once, instead of just one at a time," Jack said, sulkily. "So, that necessitated for me to reload, which cost me precious time."

"Why didn't you use the Dragoon?" I asked. I did not want to encourage better defensive measures on his part when next I came to bring him to justice, but I did not expect there to be a next time, given the crimes he was accused of. He had never killed a man as far as I knew, but he had parted so many of them from their purses and so many coaches from their strongboxes that I saw very little hope for him when he appeared before Judge Widney.

"I prefer the pepperbox to the Dragoon," he said, his forehead furrowed, as if the question mystified him. "The Dragoon is a weighty and incommodious weapon. I'd have killed you right good and proper if my pepperbox hadn't misfired."

"I wouldn't have let him kill you, Detective Harris," said Sadie kindly, again in Yiddish. "You have always been good to me."

Jack glared at her. Although I doubted he understood Yiddish, he did find suspicious the easy manner Sadie and I had with one another. "He your pimp?" he growled at her. "I wish you woulda told me your pimp was a Los Angeles Police Detective."

"I am not her pimp, sir," I said, quietly but firmly, and in English. "That is an offensive suggestion."

"Why, Detective Harris ain't no pimp, you fiddle-headed bottom-feeder," Sadie said, also in English for Jack's benefit.

"I just bet he ain't," said Jack, doubtfully.

I should like to pause this narrative for a moment here to clarify that I am neither a pimp nor a frequenter of the services of prostitutes. I am trusted and well-regarded among the Sporting Ladies of Los Angeles, but that is precisely because I am not a pimp nor a frequenter of their services, unlike several Los Angeles city and county lawmen I could name but choose not to. I endeavor to be a fair and just policeman, and while I am far from perfect, I am not corrupt.

"I never thought you'd come for Jack at Pico House," Sadie said to me, again in Yiddish, as George put our prisoner in shackles. "I thought for certain you'd be in Sonoratown looking for Tiburcio Vásquez."

George and I exchanged a glance. He did not understand or speak Yiddish, as I did, he being a gentile and me a Jew; but he recognized the name: Tiburcio Vásquez was the most-wanted man in California at that time, a price on his head of $6000 dead and $8000 if taken alive. Neither one of us had known he was in Los Angeles.

"Well," I replied to Sadie, also in Yiddish. "We can't be everywhere all at once, can we?"

"I suppose his girl must have paid you off, you damn pimp," Jack grumbled. He too recognized the name Tiburcio Vásquez amidst the Yiddish. Tiburcio Vásquez was the name that was on everybody's lips in the Spring of that year. "I guess if *la Coneja* paid me off, I'd look the other way, too."

La Coneja was a renowned Californio beauty and Sporting Woman who worked out of Sonoratown. She was rumored to be the favorite of Vásquez, who was renowned as much for his amorousness as his outlawry.

George and I exchanged another glance.

George raised an eyebrow.

I thought it over.

Perhaps it was the lack of sleep interfering with my sober judgement; we had staked out the Bell Union Hotel all the last night previous, in the mistaken belief that Three-Fingered Jack was staying there. Then, when we discovered our error, we had spent all the day and into the next evening setting about to correct it and find our fugitive. So, we had not slept and perhaps should not have made the decision that we did.

But we made it.

I looked at George and nodded my agreement.

George unlocked one of the shackles that bound Jack's wrists, strung the chain through the headboard, and then re-shackled Jack's free wrist. The desperado was now chained to the bed frame, and it was a heavy one – not one likely to be broken by a man with eight fingers or even one with all ten.

"What's all this about?" Jack inquired.

"We'll be taking these, Jack," I said, gathering up his weapons. "We hope you've learned your lesson. A life of crime and excess can only lead to ruination."

Jack shrugged. "I already lost two fingers to a life of crime," he said. "I guess you're right at that."

"We will be back to take you to the jail house," I said. "But first we have some business to attend to in Sonoratown."

Three-Fingered Jack was a worthy arrest, but Tiburcio Vásquez was another thing entirely.

It was a fine Spring evening as we made our way to Sonoratown, our boots back upon our feet. Sonoratown was only a block North of Pico House, which was in turn on the *Plaza de Los Ángeles*. The scent of primrose, nightshade, and California buckeye wafted by on a temperate breeze, competing with the brine off the Pacific, and with the stench of horse piss and beer, odors which pervaded much of the city.

Sonoratown was a neighborhood of mostly old adobe houses, many of them from the days before the American conquest when the flag of Mexico still flew above *el Pueblo de Nuestra Señora la Reina de los Ángeles*, or the Town of Our Lady the Queen of the Angels, as it was then known. The neighborhood got its name from the flood of Mexicans who went North to pan for gold, and who returned South when their claims went bust, or when they were kicked off their claims by unscrupulous whites. Many returned to Mexico, but some settled in Los Angeles, in the neighborhood North of the Plaza. Not all the Mexican 49ers were from Sonora, but many of them were. They joined the Californios, the original California-born Mexican residents, already living there.

The Sonoratown residents were naturally suspicious of

whites, and I could not blame them. But even here, I had my confidants.

At the intersection of Ord and North Main Street, George waited outside while I stepped into *Diego's Cantina,* and greeted its proprietor, Diego Salinas, a Mexican Jew, in Ladino, the language of Jews from Spanish-speaking countries.

I speak English, Spanish, Yiddish, and Ladino. I am also friendly with the residents of Chinatown, whose persons I attempted to defend, with only partial success, during the horrific Chinatown Massacre in 1871, although I do not speak their languages. These associations, of language and friendship, have assisted me in securing the return of stolen goods and apprehending fugitives, because there is always someone from one of those communities who knows something useful.

Securing information that would lead us to the capture of Vásquez, however would prove unusually elusive.

"I know why you're here, Detective," Diego said.

"Why am I here then, friend?" I replied.

"You are here to find Tiburcio Vásquez."

I frowned. "Does everybody know where Vásquez is hiding except for the Los Angeles police?"

Diego shrugged. "Everyone in Sonoratown does. And not one of them will tell you where he's hiding. Vásquez is a great hero to everyone here. He defends the rights of Sonorans, Mexicans, and Californios against the oppression of the *norteamericanos.*"

This perplexed me. "He's a common highwayman," I said.

Diego raised an eyebrow. "What is the conquest of California by the *norteamericanos* if not common highway robbery, dressed up in flags and banners?"

When California became American, I was still in Prussia, and barely a decade into my life, so I did not have deeply considered opinions on the subject. Still, I could imagine that what to me, a poor Jewish immigrant from Europe, had seemed like the land of opportunity could well have seemed like a stolen opportunity to a poor Jewish immigrant from Sonora like Diego.

"I suppose this means you are declining to tell me where he is hiding?" I said.

"I cannot," Diego said, sadly. "I also hope you will take your leave of Sonoratown and refrain from seeking him out. He is an excellent marksman and has escaped many a lawman's best efforts."

"You know I cannot do that, Diego," I said.

"Then I wish you good health, my friend," Diego said. "But I cannot wish you success in this endeavor. Even so, I hope you come through it unscathed."

"Why, that damn Sonoran swindler," George said, when I reported my conversation with Diego. "Why, we oughtta place him under arrest for the obstruction of the execution of our lawful duties."

"Never mind about that," I said. "If we don't know where to find Vásquez, I think I know where we can find *la Coneja.* Perhaps one will lead to the other."

We were only a few blocks from *Diego's Cantina* when we were accosted by both City Marshal William C. Warren -- who was not only in charge of the by-now-twelve-man Los Angeles police department, but who also had the dubious distinction of being both a scoundrel and a fool -- alongside Special Officer Joseph Franklin Dye, who was among one of the most unscrupulous characters yet to serve as a Los Angeles policeman. Dye had been a member of the murderous Mason-Henry Gang during the War, and as a policeman cared much more for reward money than he did for his civic duty.

They were accompanied by Warren's sycophantic deputy, Jacob F. Jerkins, a small bespectacled man with a talent for taking notes and saying, "yes sir."

"Now see here, Harris and Garde, what are you doing in Sonoratown?" Marshal Warren demanded.

Jerkins looked at us severely, aping his superior's disposition.

"We are patrolling the streets, and keeping the peace," I said. "I believe that is in our job description."

"Well, get the hell out of Sonoratown," Dye said, waving his walking stick at us menacingly. "If you know what's good for you."

I did not relish being threatened by such a poor excuse for a policeman as Joe Dye. I was severely tempted to snatch that walking stick out of his hand and break it over his head. But I let it pass for the sake of expediency.

"Yes, go, and go now . . . unless you know the whereabouts of Tiburcio Vásquez," the Marshal said. "If the latter is the case, I order you to share said information with me, and with dispatch."

I was not certain how Warren had learned of Vásquez's presence in Sonoratown. Warren had never made much effort to garner the kind of trust among Angelenos that would have made him privy to such a secret, even if that secret appeared to be very much an open one. I suppose it was possible he had beaten or intimidated a suspect for the information. Certainly, if Joe Dye had been by his side, such an approach was likelier than not.

Regardless of how he had come about it, here he was.

"I do not know the whereabouts of Tiburcio Vásquez," I said, which was not a lie -- I did not know where Vásquez was hiding . . . even if I had a pretty good idea where to find *la Coneja*. "Do you have reason to believe he is in Sonoratown?" I asked, innocently.

"Of course not!" Marshal Warren exclaimed, his bluster insufficient to mask his evident insincerity.

"You'd better not get in our way, Harris," Dye said, waving his walking stick again. "If you know what's good for you!"

At that moment I felt what would have been most good for me was to punch Joe Dye in his bullying face, but I resisted.

"Get in your way?" I asked, tamping down my wroth and playing the innocent. "Get in your way whilst you are doing *what*, exactly?"

Warren and Dye exchanged glances.

"You just move yourselves on out of Sonoratown," the Marshal said.

"Yes sir," I said.

They began to move down Ord Street together, Dye turning around periodically to glower at me and wave his walking stick threateningly, while Jerkins turned to wag a finger at me menacingly.

We waited until they had turned a corner and disappeared.

"They are going in the wrong direction," I said. "Let's get moving before they figure that out."

"Then we're not leaving Sonoratown?" George asked.

"Certainly not," I said. "Law must be enforced, and justice upheld. We can't rely on *that* trio to do it, can we?"

We reached our destination and walked quietly down a dimly-lantern-lit alleyway towards one of the few two-storied adobes in the neighborhood, in which I believed *la Coneja* to reside. Despite our stealth, however, a second-floor window opened, a pistol that appeared to be a Navy Colt manifested itself, and two shots were fired in quick succession, blowing out clods of dirt at our feet, leaving billowing dust clouds in the street before us.

George and I drew our weapons and returned fire clumsily as we charged towards the elevated wooden sidewalk to our right, taking cover behind some formidable wooden barrels, filled with what we knew not, but which we hoped would prove adequate to our purpose.

"Emile Harris?" called a voice from the second floor.

George looked at me in perplexity. "Vásquez knows you by name?" he said.

"I've never met the man," I said.

"Emile Harris?" the voice repeated. "My name is Tiburcio Vásquez." He spoke with elegant diction and an upper-class Californio accent.

"I know your name," I said. "We wouldn't be here if we didn't know who you are. How do you know me?"

"*La Coneja* has only kind things to say about you," he called. "She says unlike your partner, George Garde, you are neither corrupt nor stupid."

"Hey!" George cried. "I ain't corrupt at all! You tell him that, Emile! Tell him I ain't never took no dime I wasn't owed proper!"

I bade George to maintain his silence.

"I appreciate *la Coneja*'s compliments," I said, "but how does that bear upon our present circumstances?"

"I would like to appeal to you on a more elevated level than that with which banditos and lawmen typically converse," he said. "You are a Jew, I am told?"

"You are correct," I confirmed.

"Then surely, you must see the parallels between the story of your Judah Maccabeus and my own struggle?" he said.

I was surprised and somewhat flattered that Vásquez knew anything at all of the traditions of my people. I wondered for a moment why he attempted to appeal to me through the story of Hanukkah, which was still far off in the coming Fall, instead of *Pesach*, or Passover, which was just around the corner, as we were already well into the Spring. Perhaps he was not familiar with the Jewish calendar; or perhaps he simply found the story of Judah Maccabeus a closer parallel.

Either way, flattered as I was, I found such a parallel to be a bit of a stretch, and I told him so.

"But Emile," he said, using my given name in a show of familiarity, "Judah Maccabeus fought against the oppressive Hellenistic Seleucid Imperial Hegemony that sought to crush not only the political independence of your Hebraic ancestral nation, but also to destroy your very culture. The story of this rebellion against the oppressor forms the basis for your festival of Hanukkah, does it not?"

I confessed to him that it did.

"Do you not see the parallels to the *norteamericanos* efforts to crush not only Californio political power," Vásquez said, "but our very identity?"

"What in tarnation is he on about?" George whispered to me.

I admit I thought Vásquez had a point, and I told him so. "How do you know so much about the stories of my tribe?" I asked.

"I am an educated man, Emile," said Vásquez. "I am not the ignorant desperado you imagine me to be, although I am friend to the ignorant and the educated both, to both the patrician and the peasant, and very generous with my *dinero* towards those in need."

"I don't imagine you to be an ignorant desperado, and I commend you on your generosity, even if you are being generous with ill-gotten gains," I said.

"But Emile," Vásquez said. "What is California to the *norteamericanos* but an ill-gotten gain?"

I thought Vásquez again had another good point, and again I told him so. "But Tiburcio," I said. "Men have been killed in your efforts."

"But not by me," Vásquez said. "Never once by me. I have never killed even one man, although I have known many that were deserving."

"But men *have* been killed by *your* men in your unlawful endeavors, Tiburcio," I said. "Which makes their deaths every bit as much on your head as on those of the men who pulled the triggers. So, even if I could overlook your theft of property and cash -- which, as a lawman, I cannot -- how can I overlook the taking of human life in the exercise of criminal activity?"

"Did your Judah Maccabeus not also take human life?" Vásquez said. "Did he not kill Hellenistic Jews as well as Seleucids?"

"Well, yes," I admitted. "But that probably was not the most prudent tactic. It led to years more conflict before independence was achieved."

"But independence *was* achieved," Vásquez pointed out.

"But only after the death of Judah Maccabeus," I countered.

"Are you saying my people will only be free after my death?" Vásquez said. He sounded for the first time uncertain.

"I cannot speak to that," I said. "But I think we both know that the age of banditos such as yourself is coming to an end."

This point was met with silence.

"Why don't we just blast our way in there, for the love of God?" George said, impatiently.

"Vásquez is said to be extraordinarily good with a pistol," I said. "Do you really want to abandon our cover?"

"Well, how do you propose we bring him in, then?" George asked.

"I am in the process of working that out," I assured him.

"Emile," Vásquez called. "*La Coneja* says you are an honorable man."

"I do my best," I confessed.

"If she comes out, do you promise she will come to no harm, and you will allow her to walk away? This conflict does not involve her."

"You have my word," I said.

George whispered in my ear. "He obviously cares about the woman," he said. "We should hold her with a gun to her head until he surrenders."

"Absolutely not, George," I said.

"You are a damn stubborn man, Emile," George grumbled.

"I know it," I said. "It is in my nature."

La Coneja emerged from the door to the adobe. She wore a colorful dress in the Mexican style, red with printed yellow and light blue flowers embroidered around the shoulders and at the hem. Her hair, long and lustrous and black, cascaded down her shoulders. She was tall and long-limbed, with a high forehead and a thin, elegant nose.

"My gosh," George said. "She is quite the rare beauty, ain't she? Why do they call her *la Coneja?* Don't that mean "rabbit?"

I confessed to George that I did not know how she had obtained that particular moniker. Then I handed him my pistol and my Henry and Three-Finger Jack's Dragoon and pepperbox and walked out into the street with my hands raised.

"I am unarmed, Tiburcio," I said. "I am at your mercy."

"I have no desire to do you harm, Emile," Tiburcio said. "Only to ensure that no harm comes to *la Coneja.*"

As *la Coneja* came towards me, I got my first good look at Tiburcio Vásquez as he stood in the open second-floor window, shirtless and handsomely proportioned, dark hair swept back on his head, a trim mustache above a strong and pleasant mouth. I could well see why his reputation as an outlaw was rivaled only by his reputation as a lover.

When *la Coneja*, this rare Californio beauty, reached me, she said, "Emile, you must not harm Tiburcio."

"I hope not to," I said. "But the matter is not entirely in my hands. Tiburcio will have to surrender if no harm is to come to him."

"Tiburcio will never surrender," she said. "He is not that kind of man."

"As much as I admire his courage," I said, "I have a duty to apprehend him."

"But he means so much to the Californios," *la Coneja* said. "He is a hero."

No sooner had she said this than I heard the unwelcome blustering voice of City Marshal William C. Warren, who came barreling down the alley towards us, Jerkins struggling to keep up, Dye conspicuously absent.

"Now, what the hell is going on here, Harris?" Warren demanded. "Who is that woman?"

"I have granted her safe passage from the scene," I explained.

"The scene of what? Is that Vásquez up there?" he said, looking at the open window. "I ordered you to tell me if you knew where he was hiding!"

"Hello, Marshal Warren," said Vásquez. "I have my gun sights trained on you as we speak."

"Vásquez!" Warren growled. "Surrender yourself!"

"Thank you for the suggestion," said Vásquez, "but I don't think I will, even so."

Warren took hold of *la Coneja* by the arm. "Is this your woman?" he shouted. "You come out here now with your hands raised if you don't wish to see any harm come to her."

"Emile!" Vásquez shouted. "You gave me your word!"

"I have guaranteed this woman safe passage, sir," I told the Marshal.

"She'll have her passage," Marshal Warren said. "When I have Vásquez."

The Marshal drew his pistol.

"Emile!" Vásquez shouted.

I knew I had to act quickly before Vásquez shot us both down, leaving only George Garde hiding behind a wooden barrel and Jacob F. Jerkins standing helpless in the middle of the alley, while *la Coneja* made her escape.

I punched Warren in the face.

He dropped his pistol and let go of *la Coneja*'s arm.

"Run," I told her.

And she ran to the mouth of the alley, turned the corner, and was gone.

Warren sat in the dirt, his hand to his nose.

"Goddamn you, Harris!" he shouted. "I will bring you up on administrative charges for that!" He turned to Jerkins. "Write him up on administrative charges!"

Jerkins scribbled angrily in his notepad.

I shrugged. "I did what I had to do," I said. "You do what you must."

"Thank you, Emile," Vásquez shouted.

Warren picked up his pistol and got to his feet. "Are you in league with this desperado?" he said, pointing to the window.

"Certainly not," I replied. "I resent the suggestion."

"You're a haughty one, Harris," Warren said, holstering his six-shooter. "We'll see if the Common Council's committee on police will take you down a notch or two when you go before them to answer charges of having assaulted your City Marshal!"

"What in hell is going on here, Warren?" shouted a voice from the mouth of the alley.

I turned and saw Special Officer Joseph Dye marching towards us, waving his walking stick in the air.

"Warren!" Dye shouted as he approached. "Are you attempting to take in the bandito without me and claim the reward for yourself? Is that why you gave me the slip at Ord Street? What do you intend to do in regard to this matter? I want my money!"

"I don't want anything to do with you!" Warren replied.

"But you have defrauded me!" Dye said.

"You're a damned dirty liar!" Warren said.

Dye had reached us and raised his walking stick as if to bring it down upon Warren's head.

Although Warren had holstered his six-shooter, he raised his arm and fired a derringer pistol he had evidently concealed in his hand.

The shot struck Dye in the forehead but seemed to glance off his skull. Dye, stunned, put his hand to his forehead and stared in amazement at the blood on his palm when he took his hand away.

The two men looked at each other, murderously, teeth bared.

Seeing what was coming, I dove out of the way.

The two men emptied their pistols at one another.

Neither man was a very good marksman, and bullets flew in all directions, all over the alley. I saw one smash a lantern. I saw another explode into the dirt right near my own head. I heard the sound of another smash into the barrel behind which George cowered. I heard a tinkle of glass from the window where Vásquez looked down upon us and I wondered if Vásquez had been hit. I saw the hat on Jerkins' head fly off with a hole in its brim.

"I am killed!" Warren shouted, suddenly.

I got to my feet and found Warren on the ground, one hand holding his groin, the other dry firing at Dye, who stood above him, dry firing back at Warren.

Jerkins stood to one side, aghast but uninjured.

I strode to Dye and punched him in his jaw, knocking him to the ground.

George stood beside me then, pointing his Whitney at Dye.

"Hell and damnation," George said. "The two of them have made a bloody mess of things."

Warren was moaning, holding his wound, which was bleeding quite freely.

Dye looked up at me, enraged. "I'll teach you to hit me, you damn dirty Jew," he said.

"You don't have to teach me," I said. "I already know how."

Then I picked up Dye's walking stick and broke it across his crown, thereby subduing him so we could take him into custody for shooting the Marshal and also so I would no longer have to listen to him shout oaths and epitaphs and insults at my person.

I instructed George to shackle Dye to a post so he could not flee, and commanded Jerkins to find a surgeon for Warren with the most urgent dispatch, for he would surely die of his wounds if they were not attended to with all possible alacrity.

Then I retrieved my pistol and my Henry and started towards the adobe.

"Where are you going?" George asked.

"I'm going to take Vásquez into custody," I said.

"But he will surely kill you, Emile," George said.

"Well, let's hope for the best, then," I said.

I jacked the lever on my Henry and marched to the front door of the adobe. I kicked it open and entered the first floor, sweeping first right and then left. Satisfied Vásquez was not on the first floor, I climbed the stairs to the second.

The glass in the window from which Vásquez had called to us was indeed smashed, but Vásquez was not in the room.

I rushed to a door at the back of the room. It led out onto a small, wooden landing, and a set of stairs that led to another alley behind the house.

At the end of the alley, I saw Vásquez, running. He had thrown on a shirt, but it hung loose and open and billowed about him as he ran.

I took aim with the Henry.

Vásquez, at the mouth of the alley, stopped, turned to me, and tipped his sombrero.

The gesture was so unexpected that I hesitated.

And then he was around the corner and gone.

Tiburcio Vásquez had escaped.

George helped carry Warren to the surgeon's and then dragged a shackled Dye to the city jail, while I returned to contend with Three-Fingered Jack.

Back at Pico House, Jack was snoring, still beside Sadie Margolis, also sleeping. Jack was still shackled to the bed.

I felt suddenly very tired. I sat down heavily on the mattress beside Sadie, taking a deep breath.

Sadie stirred.

"Hello, Emile," she said, again in Yiddish. "Did you capture Vásquez?"

I told her I had not.

I was still perplexed by my failure to pull the trigger when I had Vásquez dead-to-rights. I supposed while I would happily have taken him in, killing him, while it may have been within my *rights* as a lawman . . . it simply did not *feel* right.

However, I said none of this to Sadie.

"Are you here for Jack, then?" she asked.

I told her I was.

She regarded him sadly as he lay there snoring. "Do you suppose they will hang him?"

I shrugged and confessed my ignorance. "It depends on how Judge Widney is feeling that day, I suppose," I said.

"He's not a bad sort, Jack," Sadie said. "His breath is sweet for a desperado, and he bathes whenever he gets into town."

"Perhaps the judge will have mercy on account of his good hygiene," I said, and yawned.

"Here, lie down," she said, patting the mattress beside her. "Jack's not going anywhere."

I was tempted, but attempted resistance. "I think that would be compromising, Sadie," I said.

Sadie was, after all, still clothed only in her natural splendor.

"I promise I won't compromise you in any way," Sadie said. "I won't even touch you. I'll just lie here beside you."

The invitation seemed too good to pass up. I removed my boots and stretched out on the bed beside Sadie, who stretched out beside Jack, who snored.

"You just catch some winks and dream sweet dreams and when you awake, Jack will be right here, waiting for you to take him to jail," said Sadie.

I was asleep before I knew it and I did dream, but I don't know if my dreams were sweet.

I dreamed it was *Pesach*, or Passover, and I was just opening the door to symbolically invite inside the prophet Elijah.

And standing at my doorstep was Tiburcio Vásquez.

I told him he made a surprising manifestation of the prophet Elijah.

He agreed and then asked me if it were not true that on Passover, every Jew had an obligation to feed those in want who came to their doors.

I admitted that it was true.

He asked me if I was going to invite him inside, then.

I did, and we sat down at my dining table with Sadie, Diego, *la Coneja*, George, and Three-Fingered Jack.

And together we ate the *Pesach* meal and promised to meet next year in Jerusalem.

The End

Apprehending Mr. Howard

an Emile Harris story

a historical fiction of the American Frontier

Originally published in Frontier Tales Magazine, October 2022. Duke Pennell, Publisher and Managing Editor. Kimberly Pennell, Associate Editor.

Historical note: Emil Harris was a real person, one of the first policemen in frontier Los Angeles in the 1870s, and the only Jew on the force at that time. He later served as a Los Angeles County Sheriff's deputy, as a U.S Deputy Marshall, and, eventually, as a private detective. Sheriff Miller of Ventura County was also a real person, and Jeff Howard really was an accused murderer with a habit of repeatedly breaking out of Sheriff Miller's jail. Policeman George Gard was also a real person, Harris' former partner on the LAPD. And, finally, the "Calle de Los Negros" was an actual red-light district in frontier Los Angeles.

Despite the factual basis for this story and its setting, creative liberties have been taken.

For the purposes of fiction, the spelling of Emil Harris' first name has been changed from "Emil" to "Emile," and George Gard's last name to "Garde," in order to indicate a flexible fidelity to the facts.

It was twilight by the time we tied our horses to the post outside the Golden Eagle Saloon beside *La Prietita,* a brothel, in the infamous *Calle de los Negros* in Los Angeles, or the Town of Our Lady of the Angels, as the Mexicans called it.

Calle de los Negros is among the most notorious five hundred-yard stretches of city block in the world, rivaled only by San Francisco's Barbary Coast, but perhaps even superior to that legendary stretch of Northern Californian waterfront real estate in its abundance of vice and degradation. In 1877, that was saying quite a lot, because there was no want of vice and degradation in most cities at that time.

The air in the alley smelled of tobacco, tallow, roast beef, and horse manure. The sounds of trumpets, guitars, fiddles, dulcimers, hurdy-gurdys, and zithers wafted with the odors from the rows of shops, opium dens, gambling dens, cat houses, and drinking establishments that lined the block.

There was also a dead horse stuck half-in and half-out of the street.

In Los Angeles, when it rains, the dirt streets transform into a muddy morass, but when the streets dry again, they are as hard as granite. The horse must have expired and sank into the mud and now was half entombed and half in the open air, immovably decomposing until the next rainstorm.

Its fragrance did nothing to improve the atmosphere.

I was, at that time, a deputy with the Los Angeles County Sheriff, having had a falling out with the chief of my previous employer, the Los Angeles City Police Department. The Chief and I did not see eye-to-eye, so despite having gained a state-wide reputation as the man who captured the infamous bandito, Tiburcio Vásquez, I had found my tenure with the city police no longer bearable.

This was how I was assigned the task of apprehending the outlaw Jeff Howard, who had considerably vexed Sheriff Miller of nearby Ventura County through frequent escapes from his jail. Howard was rumored to be in *Calle de los Negros,* an area of town with which I had more than a passing familiarity.

I was joined in this endeavor by my wife of six months, Lettie Rosenfeld Harris. Lettie, upon learning that, as a woman, she could not join any of the government law enforcement agencies, had joined the Pinkertons for a time, but, dissatisfied with their practices, had with a sum procured from her father (who had made a fortune in dry goods in San Francisco during the Gold Rush) subsequently established her own detective agency, and proceeded thereafter to accompany me on many of my duties, serving as an unpaid detective consultant.

"Can I convince you to go home and allow me to handle this?" I asked Lettie. Although my wife was brave and capable, I often feared for her safety.

"Mr. Harris," she said, "what a silly question."

When working together in a professional capacity, we always referred to one another as "Mr. Harris" and "Miss Rosenfeld." Only in the intimacy of our private moments was I "Emile" and she "Lettie."

Resigned to my wife's indomitable will, I walked with her into the Golden Eagle Saloon, where we were met by the sound of clinking glasses filled with brandy, rye, and aguardiente. A large roast sat upon the bar, with a huge knife and an even more impressively sized two-pronged fork beside it. Patrons occasionally carved off a piece and ate it with their fingers. The Golden Eagle's customers largely eschewed the stack of small plates place upon the bar beside the meat.

We sauntered up to the bar and ordered two glasses of aguardiente. The barkeep served us, and Lettie wandered to the roast. She picked up the fork and knife and began to carve small pieces, placing them on a ceramic plate.

I turned and looked at the crowd as I sipped my aguardiente.

It was a rough crowd all right, although not untypical of the crowds who did their drinking in this establishment. Several of them were members of the Sydney Ducks gang, a group of Australians who had once formed a criminal enterprise in San Francisco's Barbary Coast, before they had been driven from town by the US Army almost twenty years ago. They had taken up residence in Los Angeles' *Calle de los Negros*, where they had resumed their criminal activities with somewhat less scrutiny in our smaller and less cosmopolitan town.

The crowd looked back at me suspiciously. Most knew who I was, both because of my reputation as a lawman and because I had once owned an establishment of my own in the alley, The Wine Room, which I had later moved to Main Street.

I was about to say something to the scrum of faces turned in my direction when I heard a familiar, unpleasant, and unwelcome voice at my side, along with the click of a pistol hammer.

"Emile Harris, as I live and breathe, what are you doing in the Golden Eagle?" said ex-special officer Joseph Dye.

I turned and looked at the disgraced former Los Angeles police officer who had shot dead our previous City Marshall, William C. Warren, but who had been acquitted of all charges on the dubious grounds of self-defense. He stood behind the bar, scowling at me.

His pistol, a Colt Dragoon, lay on the bar, his hand casually wrapped around its grip, his finger gently caressing its trigger, the hammer fully back.

"What are you doing back in Los Angeles?" I asked. "I thought you were in Santa Barbara."

"I missed my old stomping grounds," Dye said.

"You've done quite enough stomping around here for a lifetime, I think," I said.

Dye frowned and twitched his mustache. "State your business, Harris," he said.

"I do not think that I will," I said. "As I do not answer to you."

Dye did not lift the pistol from the bar, but he cut his head towards it. "Don't you, now, you filthy Jew?" he asked, none too politely.

It is true I am a Jew – previously the only Jew in the Los Angeles Police Department, and at that time the only Jew with the Los Angeles County Sheriff. But judging by the condition of the clothes on Dye's back and the condition of those on my own, I was not the one who could rightly be accused of being filthy.

Just then, Lettie brought the two-pronged fork down, its sharp ends pinning the sleeve cuffs of Dye's jacket to the bar top, trapping his gun and gun hand.

I saw Dye's eyes go wide in surprise as he struggled to free himself.

I punched him in the jaw. I felt the power of the blow surge through my fist and into my shoulder, and Dye's body reeled back, then lurched forward, his arm still pinned in place by the tongs. His head bounced off the bar and he fell unconscious, slumped behind the bar with his arm still attached by the sleeves to its top.

I picked up the Dragoon from the bar and eased the hammer back into place, the better to avoid any unintended discharge.

A bevy of tough customers were inching towards me with unpleasant countenances. They seemed displeased at the violence I had visited upon Dye, although I considered it proportional to the violence he had implied that he intended to visit upon me.

As the men approached, Lettie spun one of the plates that sat beside the roast through the air, and it shattered

into one of the would-be assailants' foreheads. The man --
short, bald, and mustachioed -- stood for a moment, a look
of perplexity upon his face, before collapsing to the floor.

The men looked about, unsure of themselves.

I raised my Deputy Sheriff's badge high in the air.
"Gentlemen, I represent the Sheriff of Los Angeles County,
the county in which you currently reside, or at any rate, in
which you are currently located. I recommend you all take
several steps backwards before this situation escalates into
further unpleasantries."

This was when "Duckie" Sydney Duckworth, the leader
of the remnants of the Barbary Coast's Sydney Ducks,
stepped forward.

"G'day, Emile," he said, for I am well-known throughout
the Southland.

"Hello, Duckie-Boy," I said, although he was no boy,
being at least in his forties by now, if not older. His
Australian accent, although diminished, still lingered. He
wore a natty vest and bowler over a frayed and stained shirt
which I supposed had once been white.

"What can I do ya' for?" he said.

"I am looking for a man by the name of Jeff Howard," I
said.

"Jeff Howard?" Duckie Sydney mused. "Well, you won't
find him here."

"Do you mean to say he isn't here?" I asked.

"I mean to say you won't find him here," Sydney said.

"It's an enigma," Lettie chimed in. "Mr. Duckie, you are
very enigmatic."

Duckie Sydney tipped his bowler to her. "G'day to you,
Miss Rosenfeld," he said. "And thank you kindly for the
compliment. How are you finding employment with the
Pinkertons?"

"I have gone into business for myself, Mr. Duckie," she
replied. "I found the Pinkertons objectionable."

"Well, on that we agree, m'lady," he said.

"Please do keep us in mind for your investigative needs," Lettie said. "We are the Rosenfeld Detective Agency. I am the proprietor and sole agent."

"So, you're a small outfit then, are you?" he said.

"The better to serve our clients, I am sure, Mr. Duckie, as we can devote our full resources to their inspective necessities."

"Well, should I ever have any inspective necessities, Miss Rosenfeld, you shall be the first to know."

"That's fine, then," Lettie said. "Now, where can we find Jeff Howard?"

"On that subject I cannot be of service, I am afraid," Sydney said. "In *Calle de los Negros*, we do not inform."

Lettie raised an eyebrow. "Do you mean you have been *paid* to *not* inform?" she asked. "May I ask by whom?"

"You may ask, Miss Rosenfeld," Duckie Sydney said. "But I will not answer."

At this point, Dye shook himself awake and got to his feet. He angrily pulled the two-pronged meat fork from the bar, freeing himself, and proceeded to swing at me with the prongs pointed in my direction.

I deflected the blow with my forearm and landed a roundhouse upon Dye's jaw. He disappeared behind the bar and did not rise.

This was enough, however, to provoke the crowd.

A large man, bald on top and upon his chin, but bushy in eyebrow, mustache, and mutton-chop, came at me, his gap-toothed mouth snarling. Although I am six feet tall and well-muscled, he was of a different class entirely. His biceps bulged inside his shirt, and his chest strained against his suspenders.

Despite my disadvantage in size, I retained advantage in alacrity. When he neared, I dodged to one side and drove my elbow into the back of his neck, driving his head into the bar with considerable force. His face bounced once off the bar top. He spun around, blood pouring from his nose, his eyes glassy. I struck him once more across his bald crown with Dye's Dragoon, and he crumpled into a heap upon the floor.

Lettie kept up a fusillade of crockery against the ruffian charge. Her aim was unerringly accurate, each plate spinning with precision and considerable force and striking its target right between the eyes, faithfully bringing each ruffian down.

Another man was upon me then, a tall specimen of Western manhood, his cheekbones chiseled into sharp edges with which one could cut leather, his unshaven and strong jaw jutting beneath thin, pursed lips, dark eyes flashing hatred below unkempt, unwashed, darker hair. His arms swung in a wide arc; the hand curled into a fist at the end of it aiming with remarkable accuracy for my temple.

I dropped to the floor and drove my boot into my assailant's testicles.

My aim was true and as the man doubled over, I grabbed him by the shirt collar and drove his head into a barstool. The barstool came apart in splinters, and the man collapsed upon it, where he lay still.

I leap to my feet in time to see Duckie Sydney raise a Navy Colt in the air and fire into the ceiling, which caught everyone's attention and promptly put an end to the onslaught.

Then, to my dismay, he brought the barrel of the pistol down in my direction as he thumbed back the hammer.

Returning the favor, I drew the Army Colt from my shoulder harness and pointed it back at him as I likewise thumbed back the hammer.

Lettie, I could see from the corner of my eye, had abandoned spinning crockery as her weapon of choice and had drawn both of her Frontier Bulldog snub-nosed revolvers, one aimed at Duckie Sidney to dissuade him from pulling the trigger whilst his pistol remained pointed in my direction, and the other aimed at the crowd to persuade them to discontinue their assault upon our persons.

We stood there for a moment, suspended, each of us a hairsbreadth away from killing one another and likely being killed in kind, when the doors to the cantina swung open and George Garde, my former partner in the Los Angeles Police Department, stood there with his jacket pulled back to reveal his badge upon his vest, flanked by four gendarmes in uniform, two on each side, all of them with their hands upon the handles of their revolvers.

"What's all this then?" George demanded.

"Hello, George," I said, without lowering my pistol.

"Why, hello, Emile," George said. "What brings you back to our old stomping grounds?"

"I am here on an investigative matter," I said.

"Is that so?" George said. He surveyed the scene, broken crockery and fallen men both littering the floor. He looked at Lettie and tipped his hat, a derby like the one I wore; indeed, like those we had both taken to wearing when first we were promoted to detective. "Evening, Mrs. Harris," he said.

"George," Lettie said, without taking her eyes or her aim off neither Duckie Sydney nor the crowd that faced her. "What a delight it is to see you."

George turned his attention to Duckie Sidney. "Duckworth, what's the trouble then?"

"No trouble, Detective," Duckie said.

"Then why all the gunplay and broken crockery?" George asked. "To say nothing of the men lying about with bloodied noses, blackened eyes, and swollen lips?"

"Just a little Saturday brawling, Detective," Duckie said.

"But it's Wednesday," George remarked.

"Every day is Saturday in *Calle de los Negros*, Detective," Duckie said.

George grunted and opened the other half of his jacket to reveal a shoulder harness that holstered his Remington .44. "Do you want to lower your weapon, Duckie, or do you want me to pull my pistol from its harness and see how big a hole it makes in your carcass?"

Duckie Sydney spat on the floor in response, but he thumbed back the hammer of his weapon and put his pistol in his belt.

I returned the gesture and holstered my pistol, as did Lettie with her Frontier Bulldogs.

"Now, Duckie-Boy," George said. "Why can't Emile here go about his investigations without all this hullabaloo and calamity?"

"No reason I can think of," Duckie said.

"That's fine then," George said. "Attend to your wounded, Duckie." He turned to me. "Emile and Mrs. Harris, would you join me outside in the moonlight for a chat?"

At this moment, Dye rose again, this time from behind the bar and armed with a double-barreled shotgun.

"I'll teach you to knock me senseless, you malignant malefactor!" Dye shouted.

I gripped the barrels of the shotgun and forced it upwards. Dye blasted both barrels into the ceiling.

The blast had heated the metal of the barrels and scorched my hand. I wrenched the now empty weapon from Dye's grip.

"You don't need to teach me to knock you senseless, Joseph," I said. "I already know how."

I smacked Dye smartly in the face with the butt of the shotgun, and he dropped again to the floor like a sack of grain.

After a pause, Lettie said, "I think a spot of fresh air would be most welcome right about now, George, thank you for the suggestion."

Of course, there is no fresh air in *Calle de los Negros*, not even outdoors. The atmosphere reeked of everything that it had when we arrived, in addition to the rapidly ripening horseflesh half-entombed in the street.

"Aren't you in charge of removing dead horses, George?" I asked.

"Damnit, Emile, why are you always making trouble wherever you go?" George complained as he lit a cigar and offered one to me. I accepted, then cut my head towards Lettie, who stood impatiently, waiting to be offered one as well.

George offered, and she accepted. George lit a match and we each put the ends of our cigars to the flame at once and puffed, our cigars glowing to life.

"I don't cause trouble George," I said. "I investigate it."

"Well, I can't have any of that Jeff Howard business around here," he said. He acknowledged my surprise and went on. "Sheriff Miller telegraphed Sheriff Rowland and City Marshal King. Sheriff Rowland's on your side, but King doesn't want any investigation in his jurisdiction, which is the city of Los Angeles, which is where you are, now."

"But we believe the fugitive is hiding out in *Calle de Los Negros*," I said.

"You'll have to wait for him to leave the city, then," George said.

"Why doesn't the Marshall want Howard apprehended?" Lettie asked, sharply. "Howard is accused of most flagrantly murderous endeavors."

George shrugged. "If I knew half of why folks did what they do, I'd be a hell of a wiser man. Heed me on this, Emile. If I must come back again because of this thing, I won't be the only one unhappy about it. Mrs. Harris, it's been a pleasure to see you again. Take care of your husband for me, will you?"

Lettie promised she would, and George tipped his derby again and walked off with his troops in tow.

"Well," Lettie said. "I hadn't expected the Los Angeles police to be against us in this investigation. It certainly does raise some questions."

It certainly did, I thought.

It raised the question of how much bribery was required to purchase City Marshal King.

Lettie took my right hand in hers. "Oh, Emile," she said. "Look at your poor knuckles."

My knuckles were indeed raw and bloody and swollen from all the hardened heads I had been forced to drive them into. Lettie brought my hand to her lips and gently kissed it, sending a tingle of lightning through my body, for I am helpless to resist my wife's kisses.

Then Lettie took a flask from her saddle bag, uncorked it, and poured whiskey on my hand.

I grimaced in pain.

She took my other hand and did the same. I grunted in discomfort.

"That should help," she said.

Then she looked thoughtfully at *La Prietita*, the brothel, next door.

"Are you thinking what I am thinking?" she said.

I looked at *La Prietita*. "That depends on what you are thinking," I said.

"If you are thinking you should find a way into *La Prietita* to talk to Sadie Margolis, then you and I are very much in agreement," she said.

Most women would object if their husband snuck into a brothel and spoke to a Sporting Lady who knows him by his given name. But Lettie Rosenfeld Harris is not most women.

The entrance to *La Prietita* was guarded by two conspicuously large men I recognized as off-duty Los Angeles policemen. Rather than risk another potentially escalatory confrontation, we decided the stealthy approach represented the best option.

Although generally, Lettie hates to be left out of the action, in this case she agreed to distract the guards at the door while I attempted to enter the adobe through the rooftop.

La Prietita was a two-story adobe sandwiched between a row of one and two storied buildings along *Calle de Los Negros*, with no space between them. This required me to climb to a one-storied roof, make my way along several more, and then climb up to the second story of *La Prietita*, and attempt to gain entrance from there.

I climbed atop a barrel next to the building at the end of the street, which allowed me to grip the edge of the roof of the first building on the block. With some effort, I hoisted myself high enough that I could swing my leg and secure a foot upon the roof's edge, thereby allowing me to drag the rest of myself to the roof. There, I crouched to reduce the chances of being seen and crept along from building to building until I reached the two story *La Prietita*.

Along the second floor of *La Prietita* there was a balcony, so I swung from the adjacent roof of the building upon which I stood, climbed the railing, and then gently lowered myself to the balcony's floor.

I crept along the balcony, peeking through the windows, searching for Sadie Margolis. I encountered many a salacious sight along the way of Sporting Ladies and their customers clutched in carnal embraces, but none of the women were Sadie, and none of the men were Jeff Howard.

Finally, I peeked in a window and spied Sadie Margolis, lying luxuriously upon her bed clothed only in her natural splendor, while a gambler I knew as Harvey Rappaport pulled on his boots, left cash on the dresser, and bid his adieu.

Upon Rappaport's exit, I rapped gently upon the window.

Sadie looked up with a curious expression upon her face. Recognizing me, she rose from the bed and, without bothering to hide her nakedness, came to the window and opened the French doors to the room.

"Emile, you silly boy," she said, in Yiddish, our common

tongue, "why don't you use the front door like everyone else?"

"I couldn't wait to see you, and the men at the door looked like such a bother to get past," I said, also in Yiddish.

"Come in, come in, Emile," she said, taking me by the arm and leading me to her bed, sitting me down as she went to a small table and poured two glasses of whiskey from an open bottle. She returned to me and handed me one of the glasses. "*L'chaim*," she said, and gulped down her drink.

I did likewise.

Smiling, Sadie took the glasses and returned to the table, to fill them up once more.

I will confess that Sadie's nakedness made me uncomfortable, as it always did. By now, however, I was quite used to it, as she was not one to clothe her nakedness if it did not suit her. We did a fair amount of business together, as she was one of my most reliable informants, and, I had discovered, it rarely suited her.

"Have you arrived at last to sample my services, you handsome boy, after all this time?" she asked.

Indeed, while I had visited Sadie many times for the information she readily provided, I had never visited her for the carnal pleasures she promised, although she had often offered them to me free of charge. Nevertheless, as a sworn officer of the law, I felt it would be improper for me to partake in Sadie's fleshly gratifications. Even though prostitution was, at this time, perfectly legal in Los Angeles County, it nevertheless struck me as a dicey proposition to take Sadie up on her offers.

And, of course, now that I was happily married to Lettie, who satisfied all my wants and more, the matter was entirely out of the question.

"I'm hoping you can provision me with some information, Sadie," I said.

Sadie sighed as she returned with the glasses. She handed me one, then sat beside me. Rather than gulp it, this time she sipped the whiskey, as did I.

"Again, with the information, Emile," she said. "A girl would think you didn't like her."

"I like you very much," I confessed. "But duty calls."

"And the wife beckons, does she?" Sadie said.

"You should meet Lettie," I said. "I think the two of you would get along famously."

"She wouldn't be scandalized by a woman such as me?" Sadie asked.

"Lettie is not easily scandalized," I said. "And she also speaks Yiddish."

"Well, what can I do ya' for, Emile?" Sadie asked.

"I am seeking a man who goes by the name of Jeff Howard," I said.

"Ah," Sadie remarked, "you are helping Sheriff Miller of Ventura County who cannot keep Howard locked in his jail, despite the fact that Howard is accused of murder and of absconding with a significant sum from a cattle rancher's payroll, which has yet to be recovered."

"I am," I admitted. "And I suspect the money from that payroll has been used to hire protection from the Sydney Ducks and to pay off City Marshal King to look the other way."

"Correct on both counts," Sadie said. "However, he hasn't used any of those ill-gotten gains to line *my* pockets, even if I'm not wearing any, so I have no compunction in telling you that Howard is just down the hall, since you asked." Sadie sipped her whiskey and pointed towards what I assumed was Howard's current location.

"Is he now?" I replied. "Just down the hall?"

"With a young Sporting Lady named Miranda Vega, a Sonoran of not inconsiderable beauty."

I'd had cause to meet Miranda Vega a time or two in my duties as both a policeman and subsequently as deputy sheriff, and I concurred with Sadie's description.

"But she cannot compare to you, Sadie," I said.

Sadie chuckled. "You're too kind, Emile," she said. She raised three fingers. "Three doors down," she said. "On the right."

I reached for my billfold.

"Don't insult me now," she said. "Your coin is no good here, Emile, as you well know."

"Will you accept my gratitude, then?" I asked.

Sadie smiled and put her mouth to mine and kissed me.

"I'll accept your sweet kisses," she said, "even if you remain stingy with the rest of you. Be off with you now. I have customers lined up downstairs to see me, and someone's got to line these invisible pockets, if Howard won't."

I finished my drink, tipped my hat, and slipped out into the hallway.

I counted doors, and listened outside the third, as I unholstered my Colt and thumbed back the hammer.

I heard only silence from within, so I assumed Howard and Miranda had completed their business. Although I regretted having to enter the room abruptly, I saw no other way.

And so, I stepped back and kicked the door open.

It swung wide and I stepped in. Miranda and Howard lay naked and entwined in post-coital bliss, which I had just rudely interrupted. They both sat up in shock and surprise.

Miranda Vega remained, indeed, a beautiful young Sonoran woman. Howard was somewhat less beautiful, but only somewhat less young.

Miranda's look of shock faded into recognition. "Detective Harris," she said. "Sadie is down the hall."

"Thank you for your assistance, Miss Vega," I said. "But I am not here for Sadie. I am here for Jeff Howard."

No sooner had I said this than Howard threw a bottle of mescal at me and leapt out of bed, making a dash for the door to the balcony.

I dodged out of the way of the flying bottle, but the liquid splashed my face as the bottle smashed. Mescal stung my eyes, although, fortunately, not shards of glass.

Through the one eye I managed to keep open, I aimed with my Colt at Howard's bare-assed figure as he reached the door.

But I could not bring myself to shoot down an unarmed and naked man. Howard escaped through the door, and I gave chase, wiping mescal from my eyes.

By the time I made it to the balcony, I could just see Howard's lower half dangling as he hoisted himself to the roof.

I rushed to him but failed to get a grip upon his legs in time. He swung them out of my reach and dragged himself to the roof. I nearly went over the balcony as my arms grappled with thin air. As Howard got to his feet upon the roof, I recovered my balance, grabbed the lip of the balcony's roof, hoisted myself upwards, and followed.

Howard was already well down the row of buildings, his pale body illuminated by moonlight. I took off in a sprint to try to catch him.

I reached the end of the two-story adobe's roof and leapt to the roof of the one-story next to it. I crouched when I landed, sprang to my feet, and resumed my chase.

Howard had just reached the end of the row of buildings and paused as he searched for a way to safely descend to street level.

I was gaining on him.

I saw Howard bend at the knees, presumably to make a leap off the roof, when suddenly, scrambling up to the roof beside him, there was Lettie, who got to her feet and charged at him.

Howard did not even see her before she tackled him around the waist and the two of them rolled and tumbled to the edge of the roof and then off it.

Alarmed, I ran yet faster to the end of the row of buildings until at length I stopped and looked down at the street below.

Lettie sat atop Howard, who lay upon his stomach. She straddled him, pinning him down, gripping his hair in her hand. Howard, evidently knocked senseless by the fall, offered no resistance.

Lettie looked up at me. "Hello, Mr. Harris," she said. "I believe we have apprehended Mr. Howard."

I looked down at her.

"I believe, Miss Rosenfeld," I said, "that in this matter, as in most, you are quite correct."

Lettie beamed at me, which made my heart swoon. I took the handcuffs from my belt and threw them down to her. She took them and shackled Howard's wrists behind his back.

I climbed down, and together we hoisted Howard to his feet, where he wobbled, still senseless from the fall.

"Mr. Howard, I am Detective Rosenfeld, and this is Deputy Sheriff Harris," Lettie informed him. "We will return you to Ventura County now."

"I just came from there," he protested.

"Yes," Lettie said. "That was contrary to plan."

"I'll just escape again," he muttered.

"Perhaps," she said. "Or perhaps they will hang you this time before you get a chance."

I saw a concerned expression cross Jeff Howard's face.

Lettie evidently noticed his expression as well. "It is often a mystery to me, Mr. Harris, how so many miscreants appear surprised when confronted with the proscribed punishment meted out for their own crimes," she said. "They should do a more thorough job of investigating the legal consequences of their felonious deeds before committing them, I think."

I smiled. Lettie Rosenfeld Harris had yet to fail to fill me with wonder at her boldness, intelligence, sharp wit, and courage.

I found myself eagerly awaiting the moment we could once again be alone together, and I could hear her call me "Emile."

61

The End

Three: Once Upon a Time in The City of Angels

The Sun Sets at the Hall of Justice

a historical fiction of the Great Depression

Originally published in the anthology *Crimeucopia - Say What Now?* (Murderous Ink Press), February 2022.

I was in Jake's Joint on Broadway across from the north side of the Los Angeles County Hall of Justice, eating ham and eggs for breakfast and reading the *Los Angeles Informer,* when Daphne Drucker sat down beside me and slid a small, saddle-stitched notebook in front of me, the kind you pick up in a dime store for making grocery lists.

I looked at her. "Coffee?" I said.

"Read that," she said, and picked up a slice of ham off my plate with her fingers and began to nibble on it.

"You hungry?" I asked. I called out to the proprietor. "Hey Manny! Get the girl something to eat."

Manny, the proprietor, ambled over to us at the counter, and refilled my coffee.

Manny was about twice as old as California and only half as sunny, but he kept your coffee cup filled. I had no idea who the "Jake" was for whom the coffee shop was presumably named. I had only ever known Manny to run the joint. Maybe he thought "Manny's Joint" didn't have the right ring to it.

"What're you having, Daffi?" he asked. Everyone called Daphne "Daffi," which was a laugh and a half because she was anything but. She was, if anything, kind of over-serious and a little dour at times, although she saved her playfulness and sense of humor for a select few, which, for some reason, included me, and, I won't lie to you, that made me feel pretty good.

"Just coffee for me, thanks Manny," she said.

Manny poured her a cup and moved down the counter to provide refills to the other customers. For an old guy, he moved fast, and he never spilled a drop . . . even if that was because he was too cheap to waste any.

"Hey, look at that," Daffi said, pointing at the front page of my paper. "They discovered radio waves emanating from the center of the Milky Way galaxy." She further perused the headlines. "And they say Prohibition might be over by the end of the year. And let's see what else . . . FDR says the Tennessee Valley Authority is going to bring electricity to all the hillbillies over there. And Sally Rand did her fan dance at the Chicago World's Fair."

Daffi looked up at me and smiled. Daffi didn't smile often, but when she did, she lit things up . . . including me.

I pointed to another headline. "Also, Paraguay declared war on Bolivia," I said.

Daffi frowned. "Listen to you, Gloomy Gus."

I pointed to another. "And Hitler's burning books in Germany."

She looked at me, curiously. "I didn't know you read books, Rusty."

"Sure, I read books," I said. "Some of them don't even have pictures in them."

Daffi picked up the notebook and held it out to me. "Prove it."

I took the notebook from her and flipped through it.

The pages were filled with a cursive scrawl, a schoolgirl's scrawl, written in ink of a variety of colors, including, occasionally, pink. The pages were ragged, frayed at the edges, and in some places, the ink ran, from apparent droplets of either coffee, water, whiskey, or maybe tears.

"I've dog-eared the pages to which you need to pay close attention," Daffi said.

She had a crisp way of talking, like an actress, although there was nothing pretend about her. Daffi was a hard blonde. I didn't know her age, but I knew at the age of fifteen (she'd told them she was seventeen) she'd driven an ambulance near the front during the War, so I'd have guessed her to be just to the north side of thirty. She wore bright lipstick and very little make up besides, and she worked as a secretary for the District Attorney's investigators, of which I was one. Our boss, Burton Fitzgerald, the LA County DA, liked his department's secretaries to perform efficiently and to act dumb, to file paperwork, take dictation, and not ask any questions. Daffi could file with the best of them, but I guess she was so efficient, old Fitz hadn't cottoned on to how smart she really was.

Or maybe he had. Her smarts, after all, were hard to miss, and Fitz was anything but stupid, himself.

Daffi was pretty as hell, but she never played it up, never giving smiles out to her male coworkers, or flirting with them on coffee breaks. She was serious and uninviting, at least to most.

I guess I knew her a little better than most. I knew she could be whip-smart funny, and had that killer smile, if she had something to smile about.

I read one of the dog-eared pages.

I'm not so dumb myself, and pretty quick a sinking feeling settled in my gut over what those words described. I looked up at Daffi.

"Where'd you get this?" I asked.

"Prostie roust last night," she said. "Took it off a working girl cooling her heels in holding."

I held up the notebook. "Isn't that stealing evidence?"

"That's the thing, Rusty," she said. "No one's treating it as evidence. No one's treating it as anything at all. No one wants to read what's in it. No one cares."

I read another of the dog-eared pages. "But *you* do," I said. "You care."

"Rusty," she said. "The girl is only sixteen."

Oh boy oh boy, I thought. Daffi and this sixteen-year-old prostitute were going to get me into a world of hurt. I could see that already.

"Why'd you come to me with this?" I asked.

Daffi shrugged. "Who else am I going to go to?"

"Any one of a dozen other DA investigators?" I suggested.

"But you're my favorite DA investigator, Rusty." Daffi smirked at me. "Don't you want me to come to you?"

"With this?" I said, holding up the notebook. "Not so much."

"And yet," Daffi said. "Here we are."

Here we were, indeed.

I finished my coffee and threw some cash on the table.

"Let's go see old Fitz," I said.

Daffi stood up, stifling a pleased smile. "Yes," she said. "Let's."

* * *

District Attorney Burton Fitzgerald sat behind his wide, mahogany desk in his dark-wood paneled office in the downtown Hall of Justice building on Temple between Broadway and Spring and glared at us after we brought him the notebook and explained the story it contained. Bright California sunshine streamed in through the blinds, but that didn't do anything to improve old Fitz's mood.

"This is your doing, isn't it, Drucker?" he said, looking at Daffi.

"Guilty," Daffi admitted.

Old Fitz pointed an accusatory and thick thumb at me. When he was really serious about something, he pointed with his thumbs.

Fitz was a middle-aged, balding, and fleshy man, but he was tough. Like me, he'd fought in the Great War, and like me, he'd come home with more than a few injuries and scars, the kind he carried on both the inside and the out. On the outside, he walked with a limp because his right knee was shot up all to hell going over the trenches in France. Inside, well, that wasn't my territory. You'd have to ask the man himself, and truth be told, he probably wouldn't tell you.

"Why can't you reign in your girlfriend, Rayner?" he said, grumpily.

"I'm not Rusty's girlfriend," Daffi said, pleasantly but firmly. She was a girl who valued her independence.

Fitz held up the notebook. "Do you know what you've brought me, here?"

"Yes, sir," Daffi said. "We've brought you evidence that children are being pimped out to Prescott Sterling Mills, sir. Probably others, too."

"You know who Mills is, right?" he said.

"He's a real estate developer," I said.

"He's a filthy rich real estate developer," Fitz clarified. "He's worth at least twenty million dollars. You know what you can buy in this town with twenty million dollars?"

"A lot of children, for one thing, Boss," I said.

"A lot of cops and politicians, too," Fitz said.

"Isn't that not supposed to make any difference?" Daffi asked.

Fitz sighed. "You know, when I took over this office, they told me not to hire too many Jews. Smart as hell, they told me, but troublemakers, every one of them. I'm starting to think I should have taken that advice more seriously."

Daffi and I are both Jewish, although neither one of us is particularly observant. Fitz, despite his grumbling, was not really an anti-Semite. He pretty much *kvetched* about everybody.

Fitz glared at us some more.

Then he tossed me the notebook and said "proceed carefully, Rayner. See what you can find. Keep me informed. Drucker, you tag along with Rusty as his, I don't know, mobile secretary, interview stenographer, note-taker, what-have-you. We don't dare put anyone else on this until we know what we've got. Do not make a move against Mills without running it by me first." He reached into a desk drawer and came up with a huge, ripe grapefruit. "Here," he said, tossing it to me.

I caught it, but dropped the notebook, which Daffi swiftly picked up.

The grapefruit was heavy and looked about the size of a cannonball, the big kind. "It's from my sister's citrus grove in Claremont," Fitz said. "She sends me crates of the stuff. I've got more grapefruit than I know what to do with. I don't even like the things. Taste like bile, as far as I'm concerned."

* * *

"Oh, I don't like that stuff," Olivia Daye said, sitting across the table from Daffi and me in the interrogation room on the tenth floor of the Hall of Justice as I offered her a slice of the grapefruit. "Tastes like vomit."

I put the grapefruit aside and offered her a cigarette. This, she accepted. I lit a match and held it out for her. She leaned into the flame and lit her cigarette. She took a deep drag and tilted her head upwards and let out the smoke in a long, provocative stream.

She may have been a teenager, but she didn't smoke like one. She smoked like a dame. That didn't mean much, though. A lot of girls smoked like dames, even if they were just girls. They learned how to do it from watching movies.

I pivoted toward Daffi, my match still aflame. She tapped my pack of Luckies until the end of a cigarette appeared. She brought the pack to her mouth and when she put it down on the desk again, she held a Lucky between her lips. I put the flame to the end of her cigarette,

68

and she puffed. I decided to live dangerously and conserve matches. I kept the match burning and lit a Lucky for myself, blowing out the flame just before it reached my fingers.

I took a drag, and Olivia surprised me with a shy giggle.

"You must have been in the War," Olivia said. "The way you cup your cigarette so no one can see the burning tip. Like you're still in the foxhole."

"You're a very observant girl," Daffi said.

"My daddy fought in the war," Olivia explained.

"Where's your daddy now?" Daffi asked.

Olivia shrugged. "We didn't get along so good," she said.

"Is that why you left home?" Daffi asked.

Olivia nodded.

"Where is home?"

"East," Olivia said, vaguely.

I let that pass. "You're sixteen, is that right?" I said. She nodded. "And you work as a prostitute?"

She looked down at the table between us. "I guess," she mumbled.

"You have a madam? Or a pimp?" I asked.

"I just walk the streets, mister," Olivia said. "At least, that's what I do now."

She looked sixteen, despite the hard, haunted expression on her face and in her eyes, and the way she tilted her head to let the smoke out of her lungs. Her hair was auburn, and her nose was lightly freckled. She had a small gap between her front teeth.

I held up her notebook. "This yours?"

She looked up again. "Hey," she said. "That's my diary."

"Now it's evidence," I explained. "You want to explain it to me?"

"You read it?" Olivia asked. She looked horrorstruck.

"*I* read it," Daffi said, I suppose on the assumption that Olivia would be less mortified knowing a woman had excavated her secrets instead of a mug like me. "I'm

Daphne Drucker. You can call me Daffi."

Olivia laughed, nervously. "Like the duck?"

Daffi smiled, indulgently, "Sure," she said. "If you like. This is DA Investigator Reuben Rayner. He's a good egg, don't worry. You can call him 'Rusty.'"

Olivia looked at me, big-eyed. "On account of the red in his hair?" she asked.

Daffi smirked at me. For some reason, she thought that was funny.

My hair isn't really that red – more of a ruddy brown, with red highlights when I spend time in the sun . . . and there's a lot of sun in Los Angeles. Even so, everyone calls me 'Rusty.' I guess I'm a little sensitive about it. I don't really know why.

Which is probably why Daffi, knowing as ever, was smirking at me.

"Olivia," I said, "what do you mean in your diary that you were 'sold' to Mr. Mills?" I asked.

Olivia looked at me like I was stupid. "That's what Mr. Mills does," she said. "He buys girls."

"Underage girls?" I asked.

"I think the word you're searching for is 'children,'" Daffi told me, sternly.

"What does it mean," I continued, "to 'buy' a girl as far as Mr. Mills is concerned?"

"He pays a lady named Francine Taylor to deliver him girls," Olivia said. "She mostly finds runaways, like me because no one knows us, and no one cares. She cleans us up and drops us off. He does what he likes with us. For as long as he likes."

"Where does Taylor deliver the girls?" I asked.

"Mr. Mills' place," she said. "In Beverly Hills. When he's done with us, Lucien, his driver, drops us off on the corner of Sunset and Sepulveda. Or at least, that's where he dropped me off. I don't know what Mr. Mills paid Miss Taylor, but he left me standing there with one dollar twenty-five cents and the clothes on my back."

"How long did he -- ". I hesitated for a second. I had a hard time forming the words in my mouth, they sounded so heartless.

Sensing my hesitation, Daffi broke in. "How long did Mr. Mills keep you at his place in Beverly Hills?"

"For about six months," Olivia said. "He cut me loose when I turned sixteen."

I felt a lump in my throat. "You were fifteen when he -- ". And again, I hesitated.

"When he 'bought' you?" Daffi interjected.

Olivia nodded.

"What did you do when they dropped you at Sunset and Sepulveda?" Daffi asked.

"I walked to the Hacienda Arms and asked Miss Taylor if she would hire me as one of her girls."

The Hacienda Arms was a former apartment building on Sunset that now housed one of the busiest brothels in LA County, serving an exclusive Hollywood clientele.

"What did Miss Taylor say to you?" I asked.

"She told me I looked like a filthy street urchin and to get out of her sight before I scared off the movie stars," she said. She looked sad. "I don't know why she said that. I was clean enough."

Daffi took a deep breath. "We're going to have you write a statement and sign it," she said. "Write down everything. Don't leave anything out."

* * *

Olivia did not leave anything out.

Daffi and I sat on a park bench in Echo Park, looking at a guy rowing his girl in a boat, at the foot traffic on the footbridge, and at the palm trees that lined the water, and took turns reading and re-reading her statement, while sharing segments of Fitz's sister's grapefruit.

"I don't know why people don't like grapefruit," Daffi said.

"It's bitter," I said, my eyes on the pages.

"I like it because it is bitter," Daffi said.

"'And because it is my heart,'" I quoted, showing off a little.

Daffi smiled a little in the corner of her mouth. "You do read books, after all, Investigator Rayner," she said. "You know Stephen Crane."

"I don't know him personally," I said. I held up Olivia's statement. "I *do* know this statement is going to give us no end of trouble. *That*, I know personally."

Daffi scowled. "Did you read the things he did to her?" she said. "In her statement and in her diary, both? It's like the ever-loving Marquis de Sade, Rusty. A girl of fifteen."

"When you were fifteen you were driving an ambulance on the front lines."

"Not the same thing, Rusty. Not the same thing at all. Think on that for a second. A girl of fifteen."

I didn't like to think on it much, but I guess I had no choice. "Do you know who Francine Taylor is?"

"I've worked in the DA's office longer than you have, Detective," she said. "I think I know the madam who runs the 'House of Francine'."

The "House of Francine" was what they called the whore house in the Hacienda Arms. It was popularly referred to as "the Sunset Strip's classiest brothel," and it catered to Hollywood's biggest stars, producers, directors, and moguls. It also paid forty percent of its profits to politicians and police. Off-duty cops served as bouncers and security. It was all run by Guy MacAfee, a former vice cop who now ran half the vice in LA, and had most of the police department, including Chief James E. Davies, in his pocket.

"Then I guess you also know who Lucien the driver is?" I asked.

Daffi nodded, seriously.

Lucien was undoubtedly Lucien "Lucky" Wheeler, a former G-Man turned private muscle, fixer, and bodyguard. Now, it would seem, employed by Prescott Sterling Mills.

"So?" I said. "What do you think we should do about it?"

Daffi frowned, deep in thought. "Go to old man Fitz, I guess," she said. "He said not to make a move without him."

* * *

Burton Fitzgerald wasn't any happier about Olivia's statement than I was.

"I'd pull my hair out if I had any left," he said. He sat slumped behind his desk, his hands laid flat upon it, his fingers spread open, like he was ready to spring, but didn't have the heart for it.

"You've still got some hair on the sides, Boss," Daffi said, pointing helpfully in case he'd forgotten where the last of his hair resided. "You might be able to grab a fistful from just above your ear."

"I think it's too short above his ears, Miss Drucker," I said.

Fitz opened his desk and took out a grapefruit even bigger than the last one and hurled it at me. For an older guy, he had a hell of an arm. That toss meant business.

Even so, I caught the grapefruit and held it at my side.

"Are we playing catch?" I asked.

"You two having a good laugh at my expense?" Fitz said.

"No sir," I said. I could see he was in no mood for our roasting.

"We're having a laugh, but it's not so good," Daffi said.

"You're fired," Fitz told Daffi.

"No, I'm not," Daffi said. "You'll never find a girl who can type half as fast as I can."

"You're right," Fitz said. He turned to me. "You're fired."

"No, he's not," Daffi said. "He's your best investigator."

Fitz stood up from his chair suddenly and limped to the window behind his desk, looking out on Temple Street. He stood there for a while. Daffi and I both knew better than to continue to roast him while he tried to figure out the angles.

In LA, there's always angles that must be figured out, and if you don't figure them right, they can turn out to be sharp angles and they will cut you but good, and I'm not necessarily speaking in metaphors.

"We can't raid the House of Francine," Fitz muttered. "MacAfee's got the PD and the Sheriff's office in his pocket, not to mention guarding the front door. I don't want my investigators getting into a gunfight with the boys in blue."

Daffi took a step towards him. "Here's the thing, Boss," she said softly. "This appears to be an ongoing operation. Somewhere, there's a room full of young girls – or maybe several rooms, I don't know, and I don't know how many girls – waiting to be pimped out to LA millionaires."

"Jesus Christ on a cracker, you two," Fitz said. "You've got me in a spot."

I waited a moment, then said, "what do you want us to do, Boss?"

Fitz took a deep breath. "You take in Mills, Rusty," he said. "Can you do it on your own? Because I trust my investigators, but only so much. They're not bent the way Chief Davies' cops are bent, but this is Los Angeles. They aren't angels, either. Most of them are on someone's payroll, if not the same payrolls as the cops."

"I can do it," I said, without knowing if I was lying or not.

I was pretty sure I could take in Mills, no trouble.

It was Lucky Wheeler I wasn't so sure about.

"I can help," Daffi said, not for the first time reading my mind.

"Out of the question," Fitz said. "I won't have it said the

DA's office has to rely on secretaries to do strong-arm work. It's bad enough I have you investigating."

"She's done better investigative work in the last three hours than any of your guys have in the last three months," I said. "Except for me, of course. There's no reason to think she won't be just as good at the strong-arm stuff."

Fitz spun towards me. For a second, I braced myself for another grapefruit flying in my direction. He pointed at me with his thick thumb, the tell that meant he meant business.

"You get Daffi hurt or killed, and you are finished in LA County, Rayner, am I clear?" he said.

"As the day is long, Boss," I replied.

I knew I needed Daffi's help to do this thing.

I just wasn't so sure I could keep her from getting hurt or killed.

* * *

There was no way we were going to take Mills in his Beverly Hills home without backup. So, early the next morning, we waited outside his downtown office until we saw his V16 Cadillac Series 452 B arrive and pull into his designated parking spot.

I was hoping Mills himself was at the wheel rather than Lucien Wheeler, but of course, no such luck. I could see Wheeler in the driver's seat, all right, looking fit and big and strong and coiled for action.

I knew we'd have to make our move fast.

I nodded to Daffi and stepped out of my Packard, approaching the Caddy from the driver's side, my gun drawn and held down at my side. Lucien must have seen me in the side mirror, which I had anticipated, but he saw me sooner than I'd have liked.

He had the door half open and one foot on the pavement

when Daffi drove my Packard behind the Caddy and stopped short, the brakes squealing, blocking in the Caddy.

Wheeler was half-in and half out of the car.

I ran to the driver's side door and slammed it into him.

The window made contact with his head and shattered.

Wheeler fell back into the driver's seat, stunned, groping for his pistol in his shoulder holster. I reached into his jacket before he did and disarmed him.

Daffi was on the other side of the car, holding her .22 two-handed, pointing it at Mills, who sat calmly in the back seat.

Mills was a dapper man of average height and build. I'd have put him at about forty-five, his hair mostly black and thinning a little on the top. He smiled back at Daffi and her .22.

"Are you going to kill me with a that peashooter, dear?" Mills asked through his open rear window.

By way of reply, Daffi pivoted, and fired.

The .22 isn't loud like a .38 or a .44, more of a crack than a bang, but it's loud enough, and when the bullet Daffi fired blew out the Caddy's rear window, she'd made her point pretty well. Mills put his hands to his ears and crouched low, hoping to avoid a second bullet. Daffi pivoted back and held him at gunpoint.

That girl had ice water in her veins, I'm telling you.

"Rusty, what the hell?" Wheeler said, holding a handkerchief to his forehead, from which a small stream of blood trickled, from the force of the door or the broken glass, I couldn't say.

"Did I hurt you, Lucien?" I asked, innocently.

"You slammed the damn door on my head, you whacky jack," he said. "What gives?"

"You're both under arrest," I explained.

"Ah, no, Rusty, don't tell me that," Wheeler said, unhappily. "Don't do this to yourself. This is not the way things are done."

"If you cooperate," I said. "I'll give you a grapefruit."

Wheeler looked at me like I was nuts. "And what if I don't cooperate?" he said.

"Then I'll give you two grapefruits," I said, and I took out a pair of handcuffs.

* * *

Mills and Wheeler were out on bail in a few hours, which didn't surprise me, and didn't really even worry me all that much. The prosecution was going to be the real test. Mills obviously hadn't been able to buy Burton Fitzgerald. The question was if the same could be said of a judge and jury.

It took all of the day and part of the evening to bring Mills and Wheeler in and to process the paperwork.

Daffi and I sat side by side at the counter in Jake's Joint, looking at the sun setting on North Broadway and the Hall of Justice looming above it. I ate a hamburger and drank a cup of coffee. Daffi ate chicken salad on rye and also drank a cup of coffee. She took hers black.

Daffi took out a flask and poured from it into her coffee cup. She held up the flask and looked at me, in invitation. I accepted. She poured some into my coffee as well.

Prohibition hadn't ended yet, but Prohibition had never stopped a single person I knew from taking a drink when they wanted to, as far as I could tell. Certainly not Daffi.

Certainly not me, for that matter.

I drank, swishing the coffee and brandy in my mouth before swallowing and asking Daffi, "why did you shoot out the Caddy's back window?"

Daffi shrugged. "It seemed like a good idea at the time. Why did you slam the door on Wheeler's head?"

Now it was my turn to shrug. "It seemed like a good idea at the time," I admitted.

She clicked her coffee cup against mine, and we drank a

silent toast.

"You're pretty handy with a pistol," I said. "For a girl."

Daffi chuckled. "My daddy taught me how to shoot."

"That so? I'd like to meet your daddy."

"You will," Daffi said, and took another swig of spiked coffee.

What did she mean by that? Was she planning on introducing me to her parents? What did that mean? Did she think we were courting?

The truth was, if she'd asked me to marry her right then, I probably would have. The more I saw her in action, the more remarkable she became to me.

Before I could press the matter, Guy MacAfee had slid into the seat next to me.

"Rusty," he said. "How do you eat in a dump like this?"

I saw Manny, further down the counter, look up and give MacAfee the evil eye.

I looked up at Guy MacAfee. He was well over six feet tall, thin but powerful, and towered over almost everyone. He was about forty-five, and he was one of the most fearsome men in LA.

And he was sitting right next to me at the counter.

"Mr. MacAfee," Daffi said. "What brings you all the way from your home in the Biltmore Hotel?"

"I'm glad you asked me that question, Miss Drucker," MacAfee said. "And the answer is: your boss summoned me from the Biltmore this very afternoon."

"I never took you for a guy who gets summoned anywhere, Guy," I said.

"I like what you did there, with my name," MacAfee said. "Guy' and 'guy.' Cute. Be that as it may, old Fitz had a very earnest proposition for me, which involved retrieving about a dozen women from various locations, including from the arms of some very unhappy, and very rich, men."

"You said 'women,' Guy," Daffi said. "I think you meant 'children.'"

MacAfee frowned at her. "I always liked you, Daffi," he said. "You got sass." He turned to me. "Daffi thinks she can say what she likes because she's a broad, and she thinks that means no one is going to punch her in the mouth."

"You throw a punch at her, and she'll probably shoot you in the testicles, Guy," I said.

MacAfee furrowed his brow and regarded Daffi. "You heeled, Miss Drucker?"

"A girl has to know how to dress for the occasion, Mr. MacAfee," she said.

MacAfee shrugged. "Good thing I'm a gentleman, then," he said, as he took an envelope out of his jacket pocket and slid it across the counter towards Daffi and me.

I looked at the envelope. I looked at Daffi. I looked back at the envelope.

"That's incentive for the two of you to stay out of my business," MacAfee said.

I slid the envelope back to MacAfee.

MacAfee looked puzzled. "Aren't you even going to count it?"

"I don't need to count it, Guy," I said.

"Ah, jeeze, Rusty, come on," he said. "You've been a cop of one kind or another since almost the end of the war. You know as well as anyone that no one trusts a guy who won't take a pay-off."

"I guess that's why I have so few friends," I said.

"Come on," he said. "Don't you want to eat steak instead of hamburger?"

"I like hamburger," I said, and took a bite of my hamburger.

"See here," MacAfee said, looking pained. "I've either got to pay you off or kill you. That's how things work in LA. The thing of it is, I hardly ever need to kill a guy. Everybody knows the smart move is to take the lettuce."

I held up my hamburger. "I take my hamburgers without the lettuce, Guy," I said.

"Are all of those girls safe?" Daffi asked.

MacAfee made a big show of crossing his heart. "With God as my witness," he said. "PD Juvenile Division is reuniting them with their parents as we speak."

"Promise us there'll be no more underage flesh trade in LA County, Guy," I said.

"Ever," Daffi said.

"If I give you my word, will you take the pay-off?" MacAfee asked.

"Your word will *be* the pay-off," I said.

"For Pete's sake, just take the dough, Rusty," MacAfee said. "Daffi, talk some sense into this mug."

"He's making perfect sense from where I'm sitting," Daffi said. "You stay away from kids; we stay away from your affairs."

MacAfee lowered his head and rubbed his temples. "You're as daffy as your name, Daffi," he said. Then he lifted his head. "Ok. You have my word, kids. No flesh peddling with anyone under sixteen."

"Twenty-one," Daffi said.

"I'll shoot you both right here," MacAfee said. He sounded angry.

"Eighteen," I said, quickly, sensing we were on thin ice. "We'll settle for eighteen."

"You think you can dictate terms to me?" MacAfee said. He was still angry. His thin, long face was red.

I turned to him. "Guy," I said, "today, Daffi and I arrested twenty million dollars and rolled up your child flesh-peddling operation. You're Goddamn right we're dictating terms. You can kill us, sure, and you'll have to, because otherwise we will go after every level of your operation one piece at a time. Want to see what kind of trouble we can cause before one of your goons manages to gun us down? And don't forget, we're both pretty good with gunplay, so that could be a while."

The red faded from his face and MacAfee stared at us,

blinking like someone had slapped him. "I don't know if you got sand or if you're just plain bedbug crazy, Rusty. Or daffy, like your girlfriend, here."

"The only question you should be asking," Daffi said, "is why haven't you accepted the terms and declared victory, already?"

MacAfee glared at us. You could almost see the steam rising from his ears.

Then, he shrugged, picked up his envelope, stuck it into his inside jacket pocket, and said, "Eighteen it is."

"Really?" I said. "I thought we were going to get into a gunfight right here on North Broadway."

MacAfee smiled. "It's easier to go along with you than to kill you," he admitted. "Dead DA investigators make for bad press. We'll lose some money on the young girls, but we'll make it up. We'd lose more if we offed you and had to deal with the aftermath, the reformers and the newspapers screaming for investigations and the like. This way, it'll be easier all around. I didn't like the flesh trade in the younger set, anyway. That kind of thing makes my skin crawl. So, we're done here. Deal."

He extended his hand, and I took it. His grip was like a vise. I felt my knuckle bones rub against each other.

"I better shake the broad's hand as well," MacAfee said, and shook Daffi's hand.

Daffi looked him hard in the eye and squeezed back.

"Rusty, your broad's got a hell of a grip," MacAfee said. He put his hat back on his head. "Either of you cross me again, they'll find your heads in Laurel Canyon, your torsos in Echo Park, and your limbs on the Municipal Pier. I hope that's not too subtle a hint for you."

"Yeah, that makes it pretty plain, Guy," I said.

"You two make a lovely couple," MacAfee said, and tipped his hat, jauntily. "Make sure I never hear from you again unless it's a wedding invitation."

Then Guy MacAfee, one of the most powerful criminals

in LA, was out the door.

Daffi poured additional brandy in our coffee cups. A lot of it.

"We were lucky to get out of that alive," I said, letting out the breath in my lungs. I felt like I'd been holding it in forever.

"It's a hell of a thing when you have to negotiate the age of the girls the hoods peddle in this town," Daffi said, "because you know there's nothing you can do to put an end to the flesh trade altogether. All you can do is try to limit the damage." She looked sad.

"Welcome to LA," I said.

"You're the out-of-towner, Brooklyn," she said. "I was born in Glendale."

"Drink up," I said. "I'll drive you home."

* * *

I was in a sound sleep, dreaming of grapefruit trees growing in the California sunshine, when I was jolted awake by the jangling of my bedside phone.

I reached for the phone and knocked it off the side table. It fell hard to the floor. The receiver fell from the cradle, and as I groped for it in the dark, I could hear Daffi's voice, distantly, coming through it.

When I finally got the phone to my ear, Daffi said, "get down to the Hall of Justice, now."

"What's going on?" I rasped, my throat dry.

"Someone paid Olivia Daye's bail."

"In the middle of the night?" I asked. I blinked my eyes, trying to force them to wake up.

"It's a set-up as sure as your hair is red, Rusty."

"Where is she, now?"

"She broke into the custodian's office and called me from his phone. She's hiding in a utility closet. At least I hope she is. I hope they haven't found her."

"Who is this 'they?'" I asked.

"Your guess is as good as mine," she said. "I'm leaving now. Get over there, Rusty. Fast."

* * *

I got to the Hall of Justice in double time, but Daffi beat me to it. I found her with Olivia in the lobby.

"Let's get out of here," I said, as I drew my Colt Detective Special.

Taking my cue, Daffi drew her .22.

We walked out of the building and down the steps to the street. As we turned towards our automobiles, I heard a man's voice from behind us.

"Are you Olivia Daye?" the man said.

I turned, my pistol trained on the man, and cocked back the hammer.

The man stopped short and put up his hands.

"Cover my flank, Daffi," I said. "Sweep the perimeter to make sure no one's sneaking up on us."

She may have been behind a wheel in the war, but Daffi knew what combat looked like. She squared off and swept the perimeter, her .22 at the ready, Olivia sandwiched between us.

"Take it easy, pally," the man said. He was about my height and age, but his hair was dark, and he wore a thin mustache on a boney face.

"I'm not your pally," I said. "Who sent you?"

"I work for Mr. Mills' lawyer," he said. "I have a legal document I need to serve."

He reached inside his jacket.

I brought my pistol down on his head and raked his skull with the butt, opening up his scalp. His eyes went glassy, and he wobbled. I reached into his jacket and found a Smith and Wesson in a shoulder holster. I removed it with my left hand and struck him again across the head with his own weapon, for good measure.

The man dropped to the pavement, his hands to his head, his hair damp with blood. He was conscious, but barely. I rifled through his pockets and found another cash-stuffed envelope, not unlike the one Guy MacAfee had tried to fob off on us.

"That was what I was reaching for, not the iron," he protested, weakly.

"You were going to pay her to recant her accusations against Mills?" I asked. "What if she refused?"

The man didn't answer.

"That was what the Smith and Wesson was for," I answered for him.

I threw the envelope at him, and the cash scattered, fluttering around in the light breeze like autumn leaves.

"You sure do have an antagonistic relationship with money," Daffi said.

"Let's blow," I said. "*Rapido.*"

"*Rapida*," Daffi said. "I'm a broad, in case you forgot."

I had not forgotten.

How could I?

* * *

Olivia rode in Daffi's DeSoto and I followed Daffi in my Packard to her sister's place in Roscoe.

Her sister was vacationing with her husband and kids at a nearby campground in La Tuna Canyon for a few weeks, but Daffi had a spare key to their bungalow in Roscoe. She let us in, and I cased the joint, locking all the doors and windows.

"I'm scared," Olivia said. She was shaking.

Daffi sat her down at the kitchen table, retrieved the

secret stash of booze from behind the bookcase, and poured Olivia a shot of brandy.

"Drink that," Daffi commanded. "Drink it all and drink it fast."

Olivia did as commanded. The brandy went down without too much trouble but left her coughing and sputtering in her chair.

"Oh cripes!" she cried. "That's worse than grapefruit."

Daffi made her down another. She coughed and sputtered some more, but the brandy had the desired soothing effect.

"Better?" Daffi said.

Olivia nodded. "Better," she said.

"Don't worry," I said. "We'll get you through this."

"I can't go back to my father," Olivia blurted out, suddenly.

Daffi and I exchanged a glance.

"You don't have to go back to him," Daffi said. "Do you want to tell me why?"

"I can't, that's all," Olivia said. The booze made her cheeks rosy, but she had a blanched look on her face when it came to the subject of her father.

"Is it because you're ashamed of what happened to you?" Daffi said. "If it is, don't be. You didn't do anything wrong."

"That's not it," Daffi said. "My dad . . . he's no good."

"No good in what way?" Daffi asked.

"I mean . . . he's no better than Mr. Mills, even if he don't got the same kinda scratch."

That was a lot to take in, and neither Daffi nor I pressed the matter.

Olivia said she was feeling tired, and who could blame her? It had been a hell of a night, and now it was almost morning. Olivia went to bed in the kids' room, and Daffi and I opened a bottle of Scotch and sat in the living room making a large dent in it.

"That girl's been through a hell of a lot," I said.

"What are we going to do with her?" Daffi asked. "Where's she going to go when all this is done?"

"One step at a time," I said. "Let's get her through the trial, then figure out the rest of it."

"Can you stay the night?" Daffi asked. "What's left of it?" I almost choked on the Scotch.

"Not in *that* way," Daffi said, sternly. "For protection."

I coughed and sputtered and cleared my throat, which burned from the whisky.

"Of course," I said. "That's what I thought you meant."

* * *

I stayed the rest of the night, what few hours of it remained, dozing on the couch, my pistol in my hand, and the Smith and Wesson I'd confiscated from the man on Temple Street lying within reach on the armrest beside me.

* * *

At a pre-trial hearing in the morning, Burton Fitzgerald dropped all charges against Prescott Sterling Mills and Lucien Wheeler.

The court room exploded into uproar. The morning papers had gone to town on the Mills story and the room was packed with reporters and onlookers eager to see a rich man get his comeuppance in the middle of an economic depression.

No such luck. The court watchers jumped to their feet. Reporters dashed for the doors to call in their stories. Citizens shouted their disbelief and disapproval of the proceedings. The judge, a lean, bald, bespectacled man, banged his gavel with increasing force, ineffectually.

I tried to make my way through the crowd to confront Fitz, but the throng of people was too thick and by the time I made it to the prosecutor's table, my boss had limped out a side door, and the bailiff blocked my way.

I turned on my heel to follow the reporters out the door and fight my way to Fitz's office but standing there in front of me was Lucien Wheeler, a bandage on his forehead, and a mean expression on his face.

Before I had a chance to say something clever, he punched me in the gut.

Wheeler was a strong man. The air fled my lungs, and I doubled over.

He didn't say a word, just walked away, leaving me gasping for breath and trying not to throw up.

I guess I was fortunate the room was so crowded, and he didn't have space to properly wind up for the gut-punch he'd delivered. I'm a pretty big guy, six feet tall and I've maintained my fighting weight since the end of the War.

But Lucky Wheeler threw a hell of a punch.

* * *

After having my guts punched out, I needed some air, so I postponed going to the DA's office to confront Fitz, and I went outside to the street.

I found Daffi standing on the sidewalk in front of the Hall of Justice. She was staring off into the distance, above the buildings and into the blue California sky, as if she could make sense of all this if she kept looking long enough.

She turned to me. "What happened?"

I shrugged. My breath was back, and I wasn't in danger of losing my breakfast anymore, but my belly hurt like hell, and even the gesture of shrugging made it hurt worse.

"Let's find out," I said.

* * *

Rosie, Fitz's stern and terrifying receptionist and gatekeeper, told us he was not available, but we brushed by her and barged into his office, anyway, Rosie on our heels.

Fitz looked up at us from his desk in surprise.

People did not normally defy Rosie.

Fitz nodded and continued to peel yet another gigantic grapefruit that sat on his desk. Rosie quietly withdrew and shut the door behind her.

"I don't want to hear it," Fitz said. He popped a segment of grapefruit into his mouth and chewed. His face screwed up momentarily at the bitterness.

"We had him dead-to-rights, Boss," I said.

"How old are you, Rusty?" Fitz said, chewing.

"What has that got to do with it?" I asked.

"How old are you? I can look it up in my files, but I'd rather you told me. I'm eating right now, and I don't want to get grapefruit juice all over the paperwork." He popped another segment into his mouth.

"I was born with the century, Boss," I said. "I'm the same age as the year. Thirty-three."

"Thirty-three, huh?" Fitz said. He peeled another grapefruit segment, but this time, instead of eating it, he used it like a pointer to gesture towards Daffi. "How about you?"

"I tell everyone I'm twenty-eight," Daffi said. "Which means I'm really thirty-one."

"So?" Fitz said. "When are the two if you going to grow up?"

"I don't get your meaning, Boss," I said.

"You two both know the score," he replied. "Why pretend you don't? Don't try so hard to live up to your name,

Daphne. You and I and your boy Rusty here all know one thing you ain't is daffy. You know how things work. So does Rusty. Why are you trying to change it?"

"Because it needs to change," Daffi said, quietly but firmly.

"Ok," Fitz said. "But what made you think you could make me the centerpiece of your reform campaign?"

"Because that's your job," Daffi said.

Fitz jumped to his feet and slammed his fists down upon his desk so hard the segments of his grapefruit jumped into the air. "I know my job!" he snarled. His face turned red, and a vein throbbed on his forehead.

Slowly, the color faded from his face, and he sat back down. "Look at the scorecard, for Pete's sake, you two," he said. "We got those girls out of the hands of the rackets and put a stop to the underage flesh trade in the entirety of LA county. What did we lose in return? A chance to put twenty million dollars behind bars. I can live with that. So should you. Here." He reached into his drawer and tossed us another grapefruit. This time, Daffi caught it. "That's the last of them. My sister sold the citrus grove. No more free lunch."

"I thought you knew, Boss," Daffi said. "There ain't no such thing as a free lunch."

* * *

Daffi and I sat on a bench in Echo Park, peeling our grapefruit, and eating our last free lunch. There were no rowboats out today, but there were still plenty of palms swaying gently in the breeze, like they had not a care in the world.

"What was it you said to MacAfee?" I said, as we sat there, glumly. "Why haven't we accepted the terms and declared victory, already?"

"Because these terms are garbage," Daffi said.

"That's LA all over," I said. "Every ocean breeze carries with it the scent of citrus and corruption."

"You're a poet," she said. "Or you read too many pulp magazines." She looked at me. "Do you think Olivia's safe? Do you think they're still going to come after her?"

I shook my head. "I have no idea," I said.

"Will you stay over again at my sister's tonight?"

"Sure," I said. "Let me run home for a fresh change of clothes and I'll be right there."

* * *

I went home to my modest bungalow on Orme Avenue in Boyle Heights, showered, changed, and as I was almost out the door, my phone rang.

I picked it up.

"Guess where I am?" Burton Fitzgerald said.

"Spending a last nostalgic evening at your sister's orchard eating grapefruit?" I asked.

"I'm at Daffi's bungalow in Lincoln Heights."

That didn't sound good. "What are you doing there?" I asked.

"Where's the girl, Rusty?"

"What girl?"

"You know which one," Burton said, irritably. "We're going to take her back into custody."

"Olivia?" I said, incredulous. "You can't be serious."

"She's still got street walking charges against her."

"Mills goes free, and Olivia gets shafted?"

"I don't see it that way," he said.

"What other way is there to see it, Boss?"

"Where's Daffi?"

"How do you know the girl's with Daffi?" I asked

"Where else would she be?"

"Street walking?" I suggested.

"Last chance, Rusty."

"I'm beginning to think you're not the guy I took you for, Fitz."

"Sorry to disappoint you," he said. "Since the girl's not here, I'm assuming they're both at your place. I'm sending a patrol car over to collect her now. Don't try anything funny, Rusty, or I'll hit you with a harboring a fugitive charge so fast your head will spin."

I gently replaced the receiver in the cradle, so Fitz wouldn't know I hung up on him right away. I hoped that might buy me a few seconds. Then I went out to my car and headed for Roscoe as quickly as I could.

* * *

I took a circuitous route to Daffi's sister's house, in case I was being followed. Finally, convinced I hadn't been tailed, I pulled into the driveway, went inside, and told Daffi what had happened.

She looked at me like she was not at all surprised.

"They're protecting Mills, trying to take Olivia off the boards," she said.

"How you want to play this?" I asked.

She looked thoughtful. "I think it's time we did a little fishing, Rusty."

"Fishing?" I repeated. "On the Municipal Pier?"

"In the Hall of Records, dummy."

* * *

The sun was setting on the Hall of Justice by the time Daffi and I stood in front of Burton Fitzgerald with the fish we'd hooked on our expedition to the House of Records.

"So, Fitz," Daffi said, "it turns out your sister did pretty well when she sold the citrus grove."

Fitz screwed up his face. "What are you getting at, Daffi?"

"The property was valued at nine thousand and she sold it for eighteen," she said.

"The buyer must really like grapefruit," I said.

"Who doesn't?" Daffi said. "Everybody likes grapefruit. Just ask Lucky Wheeler. Since he's the guy who bought the property. For twice what it's worth."

"Lucky must really like grapefruit," I said.

"I wonder where he got the cash, though?" Daffi said.

"How the hell should I know?" Fitz growled, but without conviction.

"Yeah, I think you know, Burton," I said. "I think you know Wheeler got that dough from Mills. And I think you know why. They say no one trusts a guy in Los Angeles unless he's willing to take a pay-off. I guess by now you must be trusted by all the right people."

Fitz looked down at his desk and rubbed the bridge of his nose. He looked somehow deflated, like his bulk had sunk into itself.

"What do you kids want?" he said, without looking up. "Money?"

"If we wanted money, Fitz, we'd have it by now," I said.

"Rusty's turned down more pay-offs in the last few days than, it would appear, you have your whole life long, Burton," Daffi said.

"This is why no one likes you, Rusty," Fitz said. He looked up. "Either of you."

"I guess we didn't join your department to be liked, Fitz," Daffi said. "Too bad you did."

Fitz made a fist and brought it down on the desk, but without the force he'd had before. He looked tired.

"What the hell do you clowns want from me?" he

croaked.

"Drop the charges against the girl, Fitz," I said.

"Done," Fitz said, wearily. "What else?"

"Hire me as an investigator," Daffi said. "I'm tired of taking dictation."

"I don't employ women investigators," Fitz said.

"You do now," Daffi said.

Fitz sighed. "Done. Anything else?"

I looked at Daffi. She looked at me. We both shrugged. We looked back at Fitz.

"We'll let you know, Boss," Daffi said.

We stood on Temple Street as the sun set on the Hall of Justice. I tapped out a Lucky for Daffi and one for myself, struck a match, and lit them both.

"So," Daffi said. "The girls walk. And so do the crooks."

"Everyone walks," I said. "Everybody wins."

"The crooks win," Daffi grumbled. "The girls survive."

"That's better than it was before," I said.

"I guess."

"No sacrifice, no victory," I said. "That's what the Greeks say."

"That's all Greek to me," Daffi said. "How come the same people keep doing all the sacrificing and the same people keep walking away with all the victories?"

I took a deep drag on my cigarette and felt the smoke fill my lungs. I breathed it out slowly into the gloaming.

"That's just how it goes, I guess," I said, finally.

"That's how the men who win designed it to go," Daffi said.

"You're sounding like a Marxist."

"I am a Marxist," she said. "A Groucho Marxist."

"Me too," I said. "But I'm more of a Chico Marxist myself."

She smiled, but just a little.

"We made some progress tonight," I said.

"Around the edges," she said.

"For those girls, that's everything."

Daffi took a long pull on her own cigarette. "I guess you're right about that, Rusty."

"Let's eat," I suggested. "I'll buy you a steak."

"We better get back to Olivia, and tell her the news," she said. She sighed. "We've got to figure out what to do with that girl, Rusty. She doesn't want to go back to her father, and I'm not going to turn her loose to walk the streets. You looking to adopt a teenage girl by any chance?"

"I wasn't," I admitted. "But I'd consider it if you'd adopt her with me."

Daffi chuckled. "Are you asking me to marry you, Rusty?"

"What would you say if I did?" I asked. I didn't really think that was in the cards, but God hates a coward.

"I'd say you were just about as crazy as a bedbug and daffy as a duck," she said.

"You'd be right about that, Daffi," I said.

Daffi dropped her cigarette on the sidewalk and ground it out with the toe of her shoe. "Let's get back to Olivia and figure this all out later."

"Ok," I said, dropping my own cigarette and crushing it out.

"Let's pick up a couple of steaks on the way and I'll cook 'em."

"You know how to cook?" I asked.

"Sure, I know how to cook," she said. "Why shouldn't I know how to cook?"

I shook my head and grinned. "No reason," I said. "Just as long as there isn't any grapefruit involved."

"No grapefruit, but if you play your cards right, after we eat and put the kid to bed, we can finish off that bottle of Scotch."

"Is that the only thing that'll happen if I play my cards right?" I asked.

Daffi regarded me with amusement. "I don't think you're a good enough cardsharp to make *that* happen, Rusty," she said.

"You never know," I said. "I have a hell of a poker face."

Daffi put her hands on her hips and squared off, facing me. "That all you got?" she said. "A poker face?"

"Cook us those steaks and we'll find out," I said.

"You haven't got a poker face, anyway," Daffi said. "I can read you like yesterday's funny papers."

"What is my face telling you now, if that's the case?"

"That you want to eat a steak and polish off a bottle of Scotch. And get a little daffy, afterwards. Double entendre intended."

"Shows what you know," I said.

"That's not what you want?"

"Sure, it is," I said. "As long as we do it together."

"Double entendre intended?"

"That depends," I said.

"On?"

"On whether or not you want it, too."

Daffi scrutinized me for several moments.

"Well," she said. "There's only one way to find out, I guess. Let's go home and eat those steaks and put the kid to bed and drink that Scotch and see what happens."

And wouldn't you know it?
That's exactly what we did.

The End

Survivors

a historical fiction of the Red Scare

previously unpublished

I was naked, lying face down on the bathroom floor, hitting rock bottom at the end of a three-day drunk. My nose was bleeding, my forehead was swollen, my head was throbbing, and my ears were ringing. A puddle of vomit lay in the corner of the room.

I didn't want to get up when I heard the phone ring. I didn't want to peel my skin off the cool tile floor. I didn't want to disturb the aching muscles in my arms and legs.

I didn't want to answer the phone, but I had to, because the incessant ringing cut through my brain like a sniper's bullet.

"Hello," I croaked into the receiver.

"Silverman? Leonard Silverman?"

"Yeah. Speaking."

"Lenny. How ya' doing, buddy?"

"Who the hell is this?" I snapped, and the words pounded in my temples.

"This is Johnny Scarpinato, Lenny, that's who the hell this is."

"Why the hell should I care?" I demanded.

"You know who I am?"

"You're Mickey Rose's gunsel. Mickey Rose is the guy who runs the Outfit here in L.A. They call you Johnny Scar for short and because you like to carve up people's faces with a switchblade. So what? Make me care."

"The Mick wants to see you."

"Do you know who *I* am?"

"You're Lenny Silverman."

"Mr. Scarpinato, I'm a screenwriter. I write movies. I write snappy one-liners. I'm the dialogue man. Most of the time I don't even come up with the stories. I'm just a writer."

"Wrong. You *used* to just be a writer, Lenny. Now you're just another black-listed Hollywood Red."

"So?"

"So, you need the work."

"What kinda work could a goniff like Meyer Rose want me to do?"

"Watch you're language, Silverman. And don't call the Mick 'Meyer.' He don't go by that name no more."

"I'm not a *shtarker,* Mr. Scar. I don't do strong-arm work."

"You show up tonight at the Tip-Top Club. You'll see what Mickey Rose wants you to do."

He hung up, and the dial tone rang in my ears.

I cradled the receiver and walked out to my back yard one last time. My bungalow and property were small by Hollywood standards, but big by Brooklyn standards, and I was still on Brooklyn Standard Time. I'd managed to hold on to the place through the HUAAC hearings and all the attendant "Unfriendly Nineteen" bad press, through the trial for contempt of Congress, through the personal sacking from Jack Warner, even through the year-long jail term. But now, out of the Federal Pen five months, blacklisted, unemployed and unemployable, I'd put the house up for sale.

When I stepped outside, the sun nearly blinded me, and I felt my knees go rubbery and my stomach turn in knots. I was still naked, but my backyard was private, lined by a high fence and orange trees. I relished the space, so vast to a Brooklyn-bred kid like me, used to cramped tenements and narrow, crowded streets. I stepped into my kidney shaped pool, a luxury unimaginable to me a few years before, and walked into the deep end until the water was up to my neck. I closed my eyes and felt the cool water envelop my sore and itching skin. I considered not coming out again, sticking my head under the surface and breathing deeply. I heard the words of HUAC chief investigator Robert Strepling echo inside my brain, electronically distorted by the high-pitched microphone feedback:

"ARE YOU NOW OR HAVE YOU EVER BEEN A MEMBER OF THE COMMUNIST PARTY?"

Oh well, I thought. *Luxury has made me soft. I've become too attached to a bourgeois way of life. I've learned to value* things. *Classic fetishism.*

I floated on my back, the sun shining down on my face, and considered Johnny Scarpinato's offer. The Outfit, the Mob, the Syndicate, whatever you wanted to call it, had to be Capitalism at its worst, its most grotesque, its most exploitative, its ugliest.

Then again, so was Hollywood. Maybe not so violent, not overtly, but it chewed people and spat them out and ruined lives just like the Mob did. They did it with gossip columnists and publicity agents and fixers and heroin instead of a pistol, but what difference that make in the end? And was Mickey Rose any worse than John D. Rockefeller, than Henry Ford? *Ford?* Ford was an anti-Semite. Rose at least was a Jew, like me. Weren't the rackets just the immigrants way of getting his piece? There were no Jews or Italians on the boards of the major industries, outside of the film industry. Yes, the mobsters killed people, mostly one another. But I knew for a fact that Henry Ford killed people too. Every industrialist did. They killed people in their factories, working them to death for lousy pay. And they killed them on the picket lines. Literally. I'd been at Flynt when Ford unleashed his goons on the striking workers. I'd been at Anacostia flats when the Army attacked the veterans camped out in cardboard shantytowns. And I'd been in Madrid, when the industry-backed embargo against the Republic finally led to Franco's rape of Spain.

And I'd seen Buchenwald, where the Xyclon-B used to exterminate my people was provided by German industry.

Maybe I was trying to fool myself with all of this reasoning. Because, bottom line, I may have been a card-carrying communist, but even a communist needs to eat. And it wasn't like I had prospective employers knocking down my door. My Hollywood friends wouldn't associate with me. My CP friends, many of them trying to conceal their party affiliations, didn't dare come near me.

Right now, I had nowhere else to turn.

I walked out of the pool, into my bungalow, and upstairs to the bedroom. I dressed and packed all my belongings I had left after the last two years -- one suitcase worth of clothes. In the bottom of the suitcase, I packed the Army-Issue .45 I'd brought home with me from the war in Europe. Then I walked out my front door, into my Ford sedan, and drove off to the Tip-Top Club, and my new life.

* * *

When I arrived at the Tip-Top, Mickey Rose was standing on stage in the smokey nightclub, telling jokes.

"How can you tell a Jewish gangster from an Italian one?" Rose roared into the microphone. "The Jewish gangster's the one wearing the Italian suit!"

"How you like him?" Johnny Scarpinato said to me as he grabbed my arm and steered me toward a chair.

"He stinks," I said.

"Yeah," said Johnny. "He needs some good material."

Johnny sat me down at a table. I looked to my right and sitting next to me was a gorgeous brunette. She had dark eyes, a thin Jewish nose, and lips of a luscious red you could disappear into. She wore a tight black velvet dress, and long gloves that went to her elbows.

"You must be Lenny," she said, and I detected a slight European accent.

"Yes, I am," I said.

She didn't introduce herself. Instead, she placed a cigarette between her lips and waited for me to light it.

I obliged.

For half an hour we sat there, watching Rose blather bad jokes from the stage, forced laughter all around. Finally, and mercifully, the routine came to an end. Rose joined us at the table and kissed the girl long and hard. She kissed him back. Then he said to me: "Lenny. You wanna write some jokes for me?"

"Someone better," I said.

"How much they paid you at the studio?" he asked.

"One thousand a week salary," I said.

"I'll pay you fifteen hundred. Starting now." He reached into his suit jacket and pulled out a thick wad of cash, dropping it on the table in front of me.

I counted the cash. Fifteen hundred, exactly.

"Make it two thousand," I said.

Johnny Scar shifted uncomfortably in his seat. The gorgeous brunette laughed. Rose's expression turned severe.

"You got a lot of chutzpah, Silverman. You ain't even got a job. You're washed up in this town. You're in no position to Jew me on this."

"Make it two thousand or I walk," I said.

Rose stared at me, and then reached into his jacket and dropped another wad of cash in front of me.

"You got yourself a gag-writer," I said.

"You better write me some pretty *farshtunkener* funny Goddamn jokes, you *schmuck*," Rose said, and started to walk away. "Come by the place, tonight at midnight," he said, turning back to me. "I'm having a party. Go home and change first. Wear a tux."

"I don't have a tux."

"Buy one. I pay you enough, least you can do is look nice."

"I don't have a home. I put mine up for sale."

"Yeah, you do," Rose said, throwing me my own house key. "I bought it back for you."

Rose, Johnny Scar, and the brunette walked off.

I counted the money. It totaled $2500.

Five minutes on the job, and I'd already received a raise.

* * *

Rose's place was what you'd expect, a gaudy interpretation of old money: Greek columns, tapestries, a fountain in the living room, a huge pool in the back yard adorned by pretty young call girls in skimpy bathing suits.

The food was tremendous. Lox, caviar, the best bagels west of Broadway.

Gangland was there: they talked to me.

Hollywood was there too: they didn't.

When the party started to wind down, Johnny Scar called me into a private room with Rose and the brunette, whose name, I had learned, was Alva. We ate more, drank more.

Alva made some innocuous comment about the size of Mickey Rose's manhood, and suddenly, the Mick lashed out and slapped her across the face.

"Please don't do that," I said, quietly, in a voice almost meek, which was not the way I felt.

"What?" Rose said, staring at me with daggers in his eyes.

"I said please don't do that. I don't like to see women slapped around."

"You ever consider I don't give a rat's *tuchis* what you like?" Rose said.

"I'm asking you nicely, Mickey. As a favor to me. Don't

treat her like that."

Rose stared at me, dumbfounded. Then he pulled a pistol from a shoulder holster, cocked the hammer, and put it to my forehead.

"Do you know who I am, you little *schmuck*? Do you? Do you know what I can do to you?"

Maybe it wasn't the smartest thing to do, but I felt Mickey and I had to get a few things clear. So, I swung my arm up, and snatched the revolver out of his hand.

I heard Johnny Scar un-holster his pistol and cock the hammer back. I popped out the cylinder of Mickey's gun, and let the shells drop into my palm. I reloaded one shell, snapped the cylinder shut, and put the barrel to my temple.

"Let's get something straight here, Mickey," I said. "I've been beaten to within an inch of my life my police."

I pulled the trigger, and the hammer clicked against an empty chamber.

Mickey blinked when he heard the click, like he'd been slapped.

"I fought for two years in Spain," I continued. "And was shot through my shoulder by a fascist bullet."

I pulled the trigger again, and the hammer clicked on an empty chamber.

"I fought in the trenches in Europe, and I liberated the concentration camps."

I pulled the trigger again. Another click.

"I spent a year in a Federal lock up as a political prisoner and lost everything I ever owned paying off my legal fees. Before you threaten a man, you should make sure of two things. One: is he scared of you? Two: does he have anything to lose? Item: I have seen too much to be scared of you, Mickey, and even if you were to kill me now, my life is empty enough that death would come as no great loss. *Capishe*?"

I pulled the trigger again, and again the hammer clicked against an empty chamber. I snapped the cylinder out and showed it to Mickey.

The shell was one trigger-pull away from the hammer.

I handed the revolver back to Mickey.

"You got *chutzpah*, Silverman, that's for sure," he said. "You got balls, yes you do."

The truth was, I knew full well how many times I could pull the trigger before the hammer hit the shell.

But never let a good party trick go to waste, you know?

And if I'd been wrong? If I'd miscalculated?

Well, like I said. No great loss.

I didn't want to die.

But I didn't care so much if I kept on living, either.

* * *

I don't know if I really earned my $2500 a week. My routines were nothing to scream about. But I wrote a lot of them, and I coached Rose to help him with his timing, and he seemed to be getting more laughs, so everybody was happy.

I certainly was.

* * *

Then one day, the Mick said to me, "You got a bathing suit, Silverman?"

"No," I said.

"Don't you swim?"

"I swim in the nude."

He peeled off some bills from his roll and handed them to me. "Buy yourself a bathing suit."

"Where are we going, Mickey?"

"You. You're going. You and Alva. Up the coast, near Monterey, to a little hideaway I got there. You'll love it, a little place nestled in the pines, got a pool, a fireplace, miles of empty beach."

"Sounds romantic."

"Don't get any ideas. I need to get Alva out of town for a while. You're her escort."

"Why me, Boss?"

"Take a look at the shitheels I got around me, Silverman. Alva's a classy broad. I want someone with her who can carry on a conversation. I don't want her getting too bored up there."

"Why's she going out of town?"

"You ask a lot of questions, don't you?"

"I used to write the gossip column for *The Daily Worker.*"

"Two reasons: A, things are heating up in town, and I don't want her to see some of the business that goes down. Two, I got another little tootsie who needs some of my time."

"You're a busy guy, Mick."

"Responsibilities. They'll kill ya'."

"You're not paying me to baby-sit, Mick. That's not part of the deal."

"There's another five hundred a week in it for you, ya' *shmuckie goniff.*"

"When're we leaving?"

"Tomorrow. 6:00 A.M."

"I'll buy a bathing suit."

"I can trust you, Silverman, can't I?" Rose said with sudden gravity. "I mean, that's why I'm asking you to do this. 'Cause you're not a *farkakte zayn-geyer* like the others. 'Cause you been places. You seen the war, you seen the Nazis up close. You went to prison 'steada rattin' out your friends. You know right from wrong. You know what a *shonde* the world can be, and so you take the things around you seriously."

"Those are words of wisdom, Boss."

"Don't kiss my ass, Lenny. I don't need you to kiss my ass."

"No sir."

"I've got other people to kiss my ass. That's not what I

pay you for."

"Of course not, Boss."

"You know why I hired you? Guess."

"To -- " I began.

"Principle," Mickey interrupted. "I hired you because of your principles. Because you are a principled man. And because you are good at what you do. And let me tell you, one ain't worth a truck load a' *drek* without the other."

"No sir."

"You could be the biggest four-eyed kike egghead this side of the Rockies, and it wouldn't make a piss-pot's worth of difference to me. Because you are good at what you do. And you are a principled man."

"Thank you, Mick." I was unmoved, but smart enough to know that Mickey's praise was more desirable than his opprobrium.

"Don't thank me, Lenny. Thank you're hard-working Litvak immigrant parents from the Pale who came here to America, who stood on the deck of a ship and looked across New York Harbor at the Statue of Liberty and said, 'We will raise our son to be an American.'"

"My grand-parents, sir."

"*Vos in der velt*?"

"My grand-parents stood on the deck of the ship, Mick. My parents were born here."

"*Kish mir in tuchis*, Lenny. Either way, those aspirations have been met. Look at you. Up from the Ghetto. Decorated war hero. Liberator of Auschwitz."

"Buchenwald."

" *Kish mir in tuchis*, again, Lenny."

"I thought you said you had people to do that."

"Just stick with me, kid."

"All the way, Mickey."

"I need people around me I can trust."

"You can trust me, Boss."

"I know I can. That's why I want you at my side."

Mickey turned and walked away from me then, and I decided he was more than a little *meshugener*.

* * *

Alva and I left early the next day. She barely spoke a word on the way up. About halfway there, she turned to me and said, "Mickey's going to be with another woman while I'm away, isn't he?"

"Yes," I said. I didn't think I could get away with a lie.

She lit her cigarette and blew smoke out the window, holding her Lucky in one white-gloved hand.

* * *

By evening we were settled into Mickey Rose's north coast hideaway. Alva took the master bedroom at the back of the house. I took the guest room upstairs. I unpacked my suitcase and slipped my .45 under some shirts in the drawer.

For a while we sat in the living room, looking out the glass doors to the porch, and the beach and the ocean through the pines. We sat that way, in silence, as the sky became dark, and the stars came out. When the air grew chill, I lit a fire.

"Why are you working for him?" Alva asked, abruptly.

"For Mickey? It's a job."

"You're a communist."

"Every communist in America has to work for a capitalist somewhere. Mickey's as good as any."

"I don't believe you."

"It's the best I can do."

"I don't understand you. You put yourself on the line in front of HUAC, and now you're an errand boy for a mobster."

I lit a cigarette, inhaled deeply, and brooded over that

one for a minute.

"Listen," I said. "I'm a card-carrying member of the Party. I guess I always will be. Sometimes I don't even know why -- just force of habit, I guess. But if you ask me, 'what do I believe in?' Well, I don't know if I can tell you that anymore. After the war -- after Buchenwald -- I don't know the answer. HUAC, that was my last shot at acting like a hero, my last gasp of commitment. Right now, I'm just treading water. Maybe my politics will become reinvigorated. Maybe I'll make a lot of money. Maybe I'll keep treading water until I decide to eat my gun. I don't know. That's where we are, I guess."

She was silent, and she rested her head in one gloved hand.

"How about you," I asked. "How'd you fall into the Mick's company?"

She didn't say anything.

I can't say why I did the thing I did next, except to say that she made me feel naked, sort of *really* naked, bared to my soul, and I had a perverse and somewhat unjust burning desire to return the favor.

I reached over to her right hand, grabbed the glove at her elbow, and roughly pulled it off.

"What the *farkakte* are you doing?" she said.

I held her wrist and stared at the row of numbers tattooed on her arm.

"Is this a surprise?" she asked, calmly.

"The accent, the gloves -- it wasn't hard for me to guess. Where was it? Dachau?"

"Auschwitz."

"How'd you survive?"

"How do you think, soldier?" She spat the words at me, with cold fury. "You've heard of 'The Joy Division?' I was a Nazi whore. While the others burned in the ovens. And I made my way to America that way. First with an Army lieutenant, and now with Mickey Rose. Do you think poorly of me for that? Do you think my life has been one great *farshtunken shonde*?"

The question wasn't defensive. It was just a question

"No, of course not," I said, feeling shame for what I'd done. "Not at all."

But the way she glared at me as she rubbed the numbers on her arm was enough to let me know she didn't give a damn what I said.

* * *

The next day was bright and clear and warm. Alva and I walked down a path through the pines, and out to the beach. It was a stretch of sand dunes and blue clear ocean that went for miles in either direction, unbroken by buildings or people. Alva and I walked silently for about a mile, and then she turned to the ocean. She seemed to be staring into the horizon, her brow furrowed and her eyes squinting.

Then, without ceremony, she kicked off her sandals, and slipped out of her sweater, shirt, pants, brassiere, and underthings, dropping them to her side where they stirred in the gentle breeze that cut across the sand.

She stood there naked for a moment next to me, and then slowly started walking towards the sea.

I should have wondered if she was planning to drown herself or something, but I'll tell you honestly, all I did was look at her.

Her body bore the scars of her experience, Nazi razor and whip and cigarette-burn scars on her backside and breasts, scars that had faded but not disappeared in the last five years. I'll tell you also that she was beautiful, really beautiful, despite the scars . . . or maybe because of them, I don't know. All I know is my heart dropped in my chest, and I felt a pang of something that I once knew but now only vaguely recognized. Maybe it was love, maybe it was desire, but whatever it was, as I watched her walk into the sea until the water came to the small of her back, I ached for her in a painful way that I never knew before.

She dove under the surface then, and when she came up, she shook the water out of her hair, and turned to me, and she was smiling with a joy I hadn't yet seen on her face, and she called to me and said, "Well? Are you going to join me or what?"

I slowly undressed, trying to control the sensation stirring within me that made my heart race with anticipation, my nerve endings tingle, and the blood surge in my body. Then I was naked standing on the sand, and I bolted towards the water, and dove in below the surface.

And then we were next to one another, and she smiled at me and splashed water at me and laughed, and I reached out to her, and before I knew what we were doing, we were pressed against each other, wrapped in each other's arms, and kissing one another deeply.

A large wave hit us then, knocking us off out feet and depositing us onto the shore. We lay entwined on the wet sand at the oceans edge, running our hands up and down each other's bodies. She opened herself to me and guided me inside her, and we made love on the beach, with the sun beating down on us, the soft wet sand conforming to the shape of our bodies, and the surf surrounding us and caressing us with the regular intervals of the waves. Then she rolled on top of me, and when I saw her torso framed against the blue sky with the sun behind her head casting a halo around her wet hair that hung in her face and on her shoulders, I lost myself and I exploded inside of her, and she exploded too, and arced her back, and I clasped my hands to her and felt her trembling smooth skin broken by lines of scars, as our bodies shuddered violently in unison.

We spent the rest of the day like kids alone on the beach, running and playing naked in the surf and sand, stopping at frequent intervals to make love again and again, until finally we joined together one last time as the sun set on the ocean, casting an orange glow upon the water while the sky turned orange and red, and we exploded together as the red ball of the sun finally slipped below the horizon. Then we returned to the cabin, our clothes clutched in our hands, our bodies tired and aching and our flesh reddened, our hearts both somehow exultant and serene.

I lit a fire, and we sat in its glow, eating sourdough bread and cheese, and drinking from a bottle of Chianti. We retired to the master bedroom and fell into a deep sleep, our arms and legs entangled.

* * *

The phone call came at 2:37 AM. The bell jangled in my ear, waking me from dreams of sand and Alva, the outside world intruding on our intimate solitude.

"How ya' doin'?" It was Johnny Scar.

"What d'you want?" I croaked, feeling my hot and swollen skin on my shoulders and face.

"I thought the only phone in the cabin was in the master bedroom, Lenny," Scar said.

"So?"

"I kinda figured Alva would be in the master bedroom, Silverman."

"She prefers the smaller one."

"That doesn't sound like the Alva I know."

"I bet there's a lot about Alva you don't know."

"I bet you're right."

"Did you wake me up at 2:30 in the morning just to piss me off, Johnny, or did you have something important to say?"

"Someone tried to whack Mickey tonight."

There was quiet for a second while I let that sink in.

"Is he alright?" I asked.

"Yeah, he's Ok. But you'd better get Alva packed and

dressed and get back down to L.A. Things are heating up in a bad way."

"If things are heating up, shouldn't we lay low up here?"

"You're not understanding me, Lenny. This isn't just an L.A. situation anymore. These guys are gunning for the Mick, and they ain't gonna stop looking at the city limits. I don't know if these schmucks know about that cabin you're in, but sure as shit as soon as they do, they'll be there. So, get your hands out of Alva's panties and get down to L.A and meet us at you're place. *Capiche*?"

"*Capishe*," I said, and hung up.

I woke Alva, and we packed and dressed in a hurry. I put my .45 in the waistband of my trousers, picked up the bags and opened the door to the driveway.

Even after I saw the guy standing there, I wasn't expecting the impact of his fist when it crashed against my jaw. I dropped the bags and fumbled for my pistol, but I was falling too fast, and the blow had nearly knocked me out. I fell hard on my ass, and then someone's hands were under my arms and dragging me to my feet. Someone drove a fist into my gut, and all the air went out of my lungs. Then I felt the cold barrel of a pistol, probably a thirty-eight, jam against my temple.

When my vision cleared, I was still gasping for breath. A balding pug-ugly not too much bigger than a hippopotamus was holding Alva with one huge fist wrapped around her jaw. The arm clamped around my chest felt like a steel cable, and I guessed my assailant must have fit a similar description.

"Where's the Mick?" the one behind me said.

"You mean the Mouse?" I shot back between gasps of air, none too cleverly, but I was under duress. I felt the barrel of the pistol crack across the back of my skull.

I fell to the floor and received a kick in my ribs that knocked out whatever wind I had left in me. I could see that the one who kicked me had black, greasy, slicked-back hair.

"Got any other witticisms, ya' stinkin' kike?" the pug-ugly said.

Then he kicked me in the face, and I felt the bone in my nose crack.

"I have to go to the bathroom," Alva said.

"Shut up," the pug ugly said.

"I have to change my underpants," she insisted. "I've pissed myself."

"Let her go to the bathroom," the greasy one said.

The pug ugly took Alva into the bathroom. The greasy one kicked me in the ribs. I felt myself on the verge of blacking out. I heard the toilet flush. I heard a gunshot explode.

The pug-ugly came stumbling out of the bathroom, his hands at his throat, blood streaming out from between his fingers. He fell against the wall and slid to the floor. Alva was standing in the bathroom door then, firing a .22. The greasy one raised his pistol to fire back, but he was hit, first in the shoulder, then in the chest, and then another through his forehead, and he collapsed in a heap and was still.

"It was hidden inside the medicine cabinet," Alva said, waving the pistol in front of her, and stepping over one of the thugs and out the door. "It is good to always have a back-up plan."

* * *

Alva and I sped back to L.A in record time. When we got to my house, I took the .45 from my waistband, and told Alva to wait in the car.

I snuck around to my backyard and entered my house through the rear entrance. The place was dark and still. I walked into the living room, and suddenly, the lights flicked on.

112

I thrust my automatic in front of me and saw Mickey Rose standing there by the light switch. He smiled. I lowered my gun.

He swung at me with a fist full of ringed fingers and hit me squarely in the face. For the second time that night, I heard the cartilage in my nose break with an audible pop, and then everything dripped black, and my legs went rubbery, and my body crashed to the floor.

* * *

When I awoke, I was face down on the floor, with Mickey Rose standing above me. Someone was on my back, and I could feel a pistol barrel digging into my shoulder. Alva was standing next to Johnny Scar, who held her arm tightly.

"You *farshtunken* little traitor," Mickey said. "You pull this kinda *shonde* with me, here? I'm here in the city fighting for my life, and you and my lady friend are *shtupping* your way across the countryside? What kinda way is that to repay a *mensch* like me, ya' *farkakte schmuck?*"

"Mickey, I --" I started to say. Then Mickey brought his foot down on the back of my head and bounced my forehead off the floor. Stars exploded in front of my eyes, and I kept quiet.

"You think you're the only one with balls around here, Lenny?" he said, then pulled a pistol from his jacket. He opened the cylinder, let the shells clatter to the floor in front of my face, retrieved one, put it back in, and snapped the cylinder shut and spun it. He put the pistol to his temple and pulled the trigger. The hammer clicked against an empty chamber. Then he put the pistol to the back of my head and pulled the trigger. It clicked again.

"See what I mean, bright-boy? You're not so tough," he said, and repeated the procedure.

"Hey, Boss, be careful there, huh?" Johnny Scar said.

"*Zay shoyn shtil*, Johnny!" the Mick screamed. Then he put the pistol to my head again. "I want to hear you beg, funny-man."

"Why don't you get it over with, Mickey?" I croaked, weakly. "If you don't shoot me soon, you're gonna bore me to death with this vaudeville act you're putting on."

Out of the corner of my eye, I saw Mickey Rose's face redden with rage, and then subside. Something seemed to have gone out of him, some deep-seated primal rage, and having left him, it left him spent.

"Ah, *gornisht mit gornisht*," he said. "You're not worth the lead." He stood up and turned to Alva. "I'll wait outside in the car for five minutes. If I don't see you in five, you and this *schmuck* have a happy life together. You wanna stick with me, you got five minutes to say your goodbyes."

Mickey and Johnny Scar left the room. Alva came to me and sat down beside me on the floor. I rolled over on my back, but I was too weak to stand. She rested my head on her lap.

"I'm going to have to go with Mickey," she said.

"I know," I said.

"Do you understand why?"

"I think I do."

"But you don't approve."

"He doesn't treat you right."

"He treats me better than most."

"Not better than me."

"But you can't protect me like he does," she said. "Besides, if I go with him, I might be able to convince him to let you live. Despite what he says, if I stay with you, you're a dead man for sure."

I felt a stab of pain in my broken nose. I couldn't argue with that one. The best chance for me was for her to stay with Mickey Rose. But what about her?

"You deserve better," was all I could think to say.

"Sometimes the world makes choices for us. I never

chose Auschwitz. Hitler made that choice for me."

"Who will protect you from Mickey Rose?" I asked.

"Mickey's not as bad as he seems. Anyway, I'm a survivor. I survived the Nazis. I'll survive Mickey Rose, too."

"Don't stay with him to protect me."

"I'll stay with him because that's the only choice for us both, Lenny. And you know that."

I couldn't think of anything further to say, and I guess neither could she. She leaned over and kissed me lightly on the lips, then got up and walked out of my house, leaving me lying on my back on the floor. I heard a car door slam, and then an engine turn over, and then I heard Alva drive away in Mickey Rose's car and out of my life.

I lay there on the floor for a long, long time. I lay there listening to the sounds of traffic on the distant highway.

My nose was bleeding, my forehead was swollen, my head was throbbing, and my ears were ringing.

I lay there in a puddle of my own blood.

I decided it was time for another three-day drunk.

The End

Four: Once Upon a Time in a Fading Empire

116

Among the Soldiers of Last Resort
a poem

a historical fiction of the wars after the War

previously unpublished

you suspected

he did not suspect

you suspected who he was

so, you did not let on

and did not give him any notion

he should suspect your suspicions

it was after the war and you, like he,

had joined up with that

motley mob of mercenaries

that repository of misfits and miscreants

sent by fading Empires

to far-flung imperial outposts

the last gasp of the old order

and you, and he, and all the others

in your ragged band of brothers

it's soldiers of last resort

fighting its last gasp of retort

to the flames of rebellion and insurgency

they would take anyone

as evidenced by the fact they took you

and by the fact they took him, too

you slept in tents beside each other

you traversed swamps, the muck chest high

your Kalashnikovs held above your heads to keep them dry

you fought in jungles

you fought in deserts

you fought in cities, side by side

you lost count how many times

he saved your life

after the fifth, you stopped counting

he began to tell you stories

he began to drop you hints

of his life before

of life and death

of love and war

of cities pounded into dust

of villages burned to cinders

of civilians rounded up and shot

or worse, much worse

sent East on trains to endings unimaginable

he had no idea – or did he? –

that while he had raged

armed and armored with the ordinance

of an industrialized nation

that you had fought him

as a partisan Jew hiding among the trees

your weapons of war

what you could scavenge

from his fallen comrades

you had watched, helpless,

through field glasses from far away

that day he dragged

your mother and your sister from

your family home

you never found out what happened

to them, after he put them on that train

but you know you never saw them again

and that was why, that day

although he had been, in a way,

the best friend you had

since the war

although you owed him your life

many times over

that day, in that bar,

in a shattered city

a parrot in the corner

periodically imitating the sound

of an incoming mortar round

to such perfection

it sent the journos and mercs

diving for cover to the sawdust

covered floor

that day, as you sat at the bar

you slid your combat knife from

its sheath and slid it between his ribs

into his corrosive, venal

yet loyal heart

and as you watched his eyes

while he bled out and died

you saw in them

the recognition you thought

had eluded him, and, you wondered

had he known? All this time?

Had he known?

had he known you would be

his executioner, even as he

made his comrade complicit

because he knew then

your blood-soaked victory would be

as sour as it would be sweet

The End

Five: Once Upon a Time to Come

123

The Ballad of the Gefilte Grunts

a historical fiction of the unnervingly near future

an excerpt from
The Republic of Broken Places
(a work in progress)

previously unpublished

From the Journal of Simon "Frenchy" Horwitz, Age 18:

July 5

Every iceberg needs a *Titanic* in order to sink its ship.

This particular iceberg needed its own *Titanic* in order to sink the ship of state.

As the hours went by, more notifications popped up on our phones, and the pieces began to fall into place.

Moments before the crackup of the USA, probably while Miri and I were together atop the hill and the rest of the Eden Hollow Health and Nature Outdoor Recreation Association Family Bungalow Community members were by the lake watching the Fourth of July fireworks – in fact, seemingly timed to coincide with fireworks displays all over the Eastern Seaboard -- a series of nuclear explosions took out the entirety of the federal government, leaving DC and Arlington in cinders and killing everyone in the line of presidential succession, from the president to the secretary of homeland security, as well as most of the cabinet deputies and assistant secretaries, and all of the Supreme Court. Most of congress was taken out as well either in the DC explosions, or in targeted assassinations at 4th of July events in their home districts.

The ragged, random remnants of the government, those who survived, immediately conferred, and issued emergency declarations. These were promptly ignored by the states, which years ago had been organized into several semi-autonomous regional authorities in an effort to diffuse some of the successionist sentiment that had been building steadily throughout the country for several decades.

Some claimed the seemingly random government survivors were not so random and had secretly engineered a coup.

Others said these federal survivors simply lacked constitutional authority to take control, since none of them were actually in the line of succession.

Others suspected a competing regional authority other than their own was behind the whole thing, in an effort to create an excuse to break away from the central government and dismantle the republic.

In any case, no one trusted anyone, so even those regional authorities that didn't originally want to declare independence did so anyway, in order to avoid being subjugated by someone else's regional authority.

This all happened within a very short amount of time, before those of us too far away to hear the explosions back in DC – or perhaps only far enough away to mistake them for fireworks – knew anything was amiss.

But everything was amiss.

Everything.

As if this wasn't all disturbing enough, the next notification we received was even worse, even as the pyrotechnic display still burst above our heads, oblivious of what had occurred:

Every able-bodied man and woman from the age of seventeen to thirty-five was ordered to report for military duty at 9 am the following morning.

There was even a link you could click to find the "intake" office nearest to you.

Because we are now at war.

Miri and I were supposed to be married tomorrow. That's why we had gathered at the Eden Hollow Health and Nature Outdoor Recreation Association Family Bungalow Community with our families and many of our friends – at least those friends who would still associate with us, as anti-Semitism has come back into fashion lately and some of the folks we used to consider friends don't want to be seen with us anymore.

So, if we go through with the wedding, the war will be our honeymoon, I guess.

July 6

Yesterday, we arrived at the forward operating base, somewhere south of Saint Louis. There was no basic training, because the war is already on and everything is full speed ahead, with the New Christian Confederacy of the Nazarene Nation rapidly pushing their way north from the part of the country that used to be called "the Bible Belt" into the Sovereign Republic of North America, which basically is the part of the country that used to be called "the Rust Belt," from the Great Lakes through Kentucky and Missouri, and from the Ohio River in the East to the Missouri River in the West.

So, it's the Bible Belt versus the Rust Belt, basically.

None of the splinter republics have an air force, because when the US collapsed most of the war planes were flown to the United Democratic States of America, which is basically most of the Northeast corridor from North Carolina to Maine and contains the remnants of the US government we all used to call our own, housed in New York and New Jersey since DC was burned to a crisp. I guess that transfer of war planes is a good thing, at least insofar as the enemy can't bomb us from the air unless they want to push explosives out of Piper Cubs or something.

Which, come to think of it, could be a possibility.

There's a lot of military bases in the South, so the Nazarenes, pushing up from Tennessee into Kentucky and from Arkansas into Missouri, have a lot of weapons and equipment and are gaining ground rapidly.

It's not clear to me what is the New Confederacy's end game. Are they going to push all the way up through Michigan if they can, and join up with our backwoods militias up there? Hopefully not, because the Sovereign Republic is counting on those militias to supplement our National Guards and our newly hobbled together Republic Defense Force to defend us in the South.

Our plan, to the degree I understand it, is to shore up the Sovereign Republic forces outside St Louis and Louisville and try to stop the enemy's advance there.

We're outnumbered and outgunned. That's where this massive call up comes in. They gave us weapons and a uniform and put us right on a bus waiting outside the intake center. Ten hours later, we disembarked at our forward operating base.

There's nothing standard issue about any of our gear. Our uniforms are Dickies and Carhartt work clothes from Wal Mart shelves with private's stripes sewn on the sleeves. Our weapons are appropriated from gun stores.

We are well armed even so. In case you haven't heard, there's more guns in America than people, so it was easy to find enough weapons for all of us. But we've all got different guns – Ruger, Browning, Springfield, Remington, Savage long guns; Beretta, Smith & Wesson, Sig Sauer, Glock semi-automatic pistols; Heritage, Colt, and Taurus revolvers. I personally have a Smith & Wesson semi-auto pistol and a Savage semi-auto rifle.

I just hope with no standardized weaponry they have enough of the different required ammunition for all of us and all of our guns.

Most of us from the Eden Hollow Health and

Nature Outdoor Recreation Association Family Bungalow Community are actually pretty good with firearms. Even though Eden Hollow is a very hippy-dippy kind of place, we do have a shooting range, and many of us excel at target practice.

Of course, they tell me shooting targets is not the same as shooting people, and I am inclined to believe them.

Most of us have no particular loyalty to the Sovereign Republic of North America . . . which didn't even exist until a few days ago. But I guess most of us can unite in our revulsion at what life under our neighbor to the south would be like.

My younger brother Lenny and I both know how to shoot and how to fight. Lenny is an amateur boxer, and Eden Hollow also has Krav Maga classes. My cousin, Rosa, perhaps surprisingly, is also really good at shooting and self-defense. And in the two years since we met, my fiancé Miri has gotten pretty good at it, too.

But of course, none of us have ever faced anyone in combat, nor ever fired a weapon at another human being. Lenny and I are the only ones in our group from Eden Hollow who have even had our share of schoolyard and street brawls. And Lenny a lot more than me.

Everything seems very haphazard around here at the base, which they are calling "Camp Farty-Four," which is, I guess, a joke on what the locals call nearby Route 44 -- "Route Farty-Four." They've got us sleeping on cots in tents, one tent per squad, and eating in the cafeteria under another big tent that serves everyone on base. Showers are outdoors and they're just a platform with pipes overhead and shower spigots attached to the pipes. There's no walls for the showers, not even canvas ones, and no roof. There's no gender segregation in the showers, either, or in any of the other arrangements. We eat, sleep, shit, and shower together. This has less to do with any notions of gender equity, I think, and more to do with everyone just being thrown together quickly and without any particular consideration. They want us to fulfill our role as cannon fodder to soften up the enemy for the Michigan backwoods militias to come in after us and kill some Nazarenes – unless they join up with them, instead. The jury is still out on that.

They seem to have randomly assembled the squads based on who showed up at the intake center at the same time. In addition to me, Lenny, Rosa, and Miri, we've got the siblings Richie and Deb Lipschitz from Eden Hollow. The rest of our squad consists of Privates Samuel "Sully" Sullivan, Hank Günther, Roy Scott, Cody Knox, Luke Gossett, Benson Tiller, Angela "Angie" Chen, Trisha Vikram, and Ruby Hopper. Our corporal is Miguel "Mike" Hernandez, and our Sergeant is Gillian "Gillie" Gilroy. Gillie and Mike are the only two with military experience, fighting in some of those Middle Eastern wars a few years back. The rest of us are between 17 and 21 years old. Mike is Hispanic, Gillie and Ruby are black. Angie is East Asian. Trisha is South Asian. Sully, Roy, Cody, Luke, Ben, and Hank are all White.

By happenstance, almost half of the squad, those of us who arrived together at the intake center closest to Eden Hollow, are Jewish. Eden Hollow has a mostly Jewish membership. It was originally established as an anarcho-naturist vegan Yiddish-speaking retreat for Jews from the big cities back in the early twentieth century. It's pretty bougie now, but members still adhere to a lot of the old traditions – including mostly speaking Yiddish at Eden Hollow, mostly all the time. Eden Hollow is not officially a Jews-only community, but the fact that it is officially a Yiddish-speaking community means most of us are Jews. Our membership has grown over recent years, as more and more places around the country started becoming "restricted" again, like it was the 1930s or something. We've even had to hire more Yiddish language teachers for new members who aren't so fluent – or not fluent at all.

Anyway, all the squads here at base have nicknames, and they call us the Disco Biscuit Squad. I have no idea why. "Disco Biscuit" was a 1970s slang for quaaludes.

Maybe they think we're all on drugs.

Maybe if we were, this whole thing would be a little less shitty.

Miri and I are still engaged, but we decided to postpone the wedding. We could have done something quick before we left Eden Hollow, but we decided instead to tie the knot once the war is over, and do it nice.

Assuming we are both still alive once the war is over.

Whenever that may be.

July 7

Today they issued us our dog tags. They have letters stamped on them designating our religion, to assist in proper burial if -- or when -- the need should arise. P is for Protestant. C is for Catholic. M is for Muslim. H is for Hindi. O is for other, which includes agnostics and atheists, as well as, I imagine, Deists, Druids, Wiccans, Buddhists, and anyone else you can think of.

J, naturally, is for Jew.

This was a little bit concerning since the Nazarenes were already well-known for their vicious anti-Semitism.

"We might as well wear our Magen Davids openly, I guess," Lenny said, once the dog tags had been issued. "There doesn't seem to be any point in being coy about it."

We spent the rest of the day filling sandbags and using them to shore up the perimeter and the machine gun nests set at regular intervals along it. By the end of the day, we were all hot and sweaty and dirty.

And so, we hit the showers.

"Hey, gentlemen, where's your foreskins?" asked Hank "Gunner" Günther, standing under the showers across from the Jews in the squad.

The Jews were all showering on one side, the gentiles on the other. I don't think this was intentional, but it seemed to serve Gunner's purpose which was becoming apparent.

The Jewish men were all circumcised.

Circumcision used to be pretty ubiquitous among American men of all religions, even as recently as my father's generation. But among men my age, it's dropped to about twenty-five percent among gentiles, and less in certain communities. As it happened, the non-Jewish men on the other side of the shower all still possessed their foreskins.

It probably didn't help that all of us on the Jewish side, male and female both, also wore our Magen David's around our necks. Many of us had gotten into the habits of hiding them or not wearing them in public, with the rise in Jew-hatred, but at Eden Hollow, everyone wore them proudly. If it hadn't been for our dog tags giving us away, we might not have done so on base, but the "J" on the tags was only slightly less prominent than that Star of David around our necks.

None of us from Eden Hollow were uncomfortable with the showering situation, since Eden Hollow also had gender-inclusive public showering facilities, which have become pretty commonplace in the last two decades or so at public pools, gyms, colleges, community centers, sporting facilities, public beaches, campgrounds, RV parks, travel centers, public marinas, hostels, and the like – or at least they'd become commonplace in the more broadminded communities across what until July 4th was the nation we all shared. But of course, there are less of those than there used to be, and many of those communities are no longer so broadminded. Eden Hollow has always been something of an oasis, in that regard.

In any case, as far as I could tell, none of the Disco Biscuit gentiles using the shower facilities, male or female, were particularly concerned about their gender-inclusive nature either. What they *did* seem concerned about – or at least what Gunner seemed concerned about – was the missing foreskins of me and my male coreligionists.

Gunner nodded to Sullivan, who was showering beside him. "You ever seen so many circumcisions in one place, Sully?"

"You leave me out of this," Sully grumbled. He didn't seem happy with Gunner.

Roy, Cody, Luke, and Ben showered nearby, and observed the interaction warily but without obvious partiality towards either side. I figured they were waiting to see how it played out.

Ruby, Trisha, and Angie stood a little further away from the rest of us, and they looked on the proceedings with concern, but didn't seem to want to get involved. I couldn't blame them.

Mike and Gillie were nowhere to be found. Maybe NCOs had different shower facilities. I wasn't sure.

"Why are you looking at my wanger?" Lenny asked Gunner.

"Tell me, Lenny, you ever miss it?" Gunner asked.

"Your wanger?' Lenny asked. "How can I, with you waving it around in front of me?"

"I mean your foreskin," Gunner said.

"You mean that thing that makes your dick look like it's wearing a wrinkly old turtleneck?" Lenny asked. "Based on the evidence, no, I don't miss it at all."

"Funny guy," Gunner said. "I heard that's a characteristic of your people."

"What people are those, Gunner?" Lenny said, aggressively. "You want to make yourself plain? Or you want me to shove this bar of soap down your throat? On second thought, given your fascination with circumcision, maybe it's not the soap you want me to shove down your throat."

Gunner's face turned red. "You better not be implying what I think you're implying," he said.

"I'm not *implying* anything," Lenny said. "I'm saying it outright. You want me to go over there and demonstrate?"

Lenny took a step towards Gunner. I put a restraining hand on his shoulder.

Lenny has broad and strong shoulders. He's short but built like a fireplug. His biceps are like telephone poles.

Even so, I'm his big brother, and I'm not so frail, either. When Lenny feels my hand on his shoulder, he takes a pause.

"I got a perfect name for you," Gunner said. He scanned the Disco Biscuit Jews. "For all of you."

"Don't keep us in suspense," Miri said.

"I'm gonna call y'all the Gefilte Grunts," Gunner said.

We all took a moment to let that sink in.

"That's the most awesome name ever," Rosa remarked, brightly, beaming joyfully. Her normally wild and frizzy red hair was now shorn close to her scalp, the same haircut we had all received. But somehow on her, it continued to look untamed. "I'm gonna have that stitched on my uniform."

July 8

We got word this morning of an upcoming musical festival outside St Louis. It's called *Jewess-palooza*, and it's a festival of all-female cover bands of Jewish or Jewish-ish music artists. So, we've got Schmaim, which is a Haim cover band; the Velveeta Underwear and Nicolette, an all-female Velvet Underground and Nico cover band; Sweater-Skinny, a Sleater-Kinney cover band; Riley Smiley, a Rilo Kiley cover band; the Roberta Zimmerman Experience, which is an all-female Bob Dylan/Jimi Hendrix cover band (Hendrix wasn't Jewish, but he did record the best Bob Dylan cover ever, "All Along the Watchtower"); Birdies on a Wire, an all-female Leonard Cohen cover band; the Rock n' Roll Animaniacs, an all-female post-Velvets Lou Reed cover band; the Blitzkrieg Teenyboppers, an all-female Ramones cover band; The Rag Mamas, an all-female The Band cover band (Robbie Robertson was both Jewish and Indigenous American); The Barenaked Bros, an all-female Barenaked Ladies cover band; The Beastly Girls, an all-female Beastie Boys cover band; the Holly Holies, an all-female Neil Diamond cover band; Walk Like Egyptians, a Bangles/Suzanna Hoffs cover band; the Rock n' Roll All Nighters, an all-female Kiss cover band; Sirens of Swing, an all-female Dire Straits cover band; Three Cool Kittens, an all-female Lieber-Stoller cover band; Biters of Reality, a Lisa Loeb cover band; Excitable Girls, an all-female Warren Zevon cover band; the Tendaberries, a Laura Nyro cover band; and Bang My Gong, an all-female T. Rex cover band.

"No, you can't go to the Jewess-palooza Music Festival," Sergeant Gillie told me.

"Why not?" I asked.

"Why not? There's a war on."

"Where?" I asked, pointing south. We hadn't seen any action.

"Are you impatient to get your war on?"

"I'm impatient for the war to be over and to get back home," I said.

"Give it time," Gillie said. "And be careful what you wish for."

"The only thing I wish for right now is to go to Jewess-palooza."

"You're needed here," Gillie said. "We all are. When the fighting comes, you'll see."

Later in the barracks, Lenny and Gunner both showed up with bruised faces, blackened eyes, swollen lips, and bloodied noses.

"You two get into it?" I asked.

"You should see the other guy," Lenny said.

I looked at Gunner. "I'm looking at the other guy."

Lenny handed me a wad of cash. "Hold onto this for me," he said.

"You fought for money?" I asked.

"If I'm going to get my face pounded, I might as well get paid for it," he said.

"You won?"

"By decision," Lenny said. He stared at Gunner. "His head's too thick to win by KO."

"How much?" I asked.

"Two hundred and fifty."

I looked over Lenny's face.

"It wasn't worth it," I said.

Lenny smiled through swollen lips. At least his

teeth looked all intact.

"It ain't about the money," he said. "It's about smashing Gunner in the face."

"You got lucky this time," Gunner growled.

"Any time you want to test your luck again, go for it," Lenny said.

Gunner grumbled something inaudible and put an icepack to his mouth.

July 10

Captain Harlow stopped by our barracks this morning and demanded we all attend church services on Sunday.

"Disco Biscuit Squad has the worst attendance record for religious services in Camp 44," Harlow said.

This was the first time I realized our camp wasn't officially called "Camp Farty-Four."

"We haven't even been here a week, sir," Sergeant Gillie said.

"It's still the worst," Harlow said.

"The thing is, sir," Gillie said. "Horwitz, Horwitz, Bernstein, Lieberman, Lipschitz, and Lipschitz are all Jewish. Hernandez and Sullivan are Catholic. Vikram is Hindu. Chen is Buddhist. Hopper is Rastafarian. Scott is an atheist, Knox is Zoroastrian, Gossett is Swedenborgian, Tiller is Rosicrucian, and Günther is *Wotansvolk*."

Harlow stared at Gillie, his face getting redder and redder, trying to decide if she was putting him on, and none too happy even if she wasn't.

"What religious persuasion are you, Sergeant Gilroy?"

"I'm a Deist, sir," Gillie said.

"I don't know what that is," Harlow said.

"Neither do most Deists, sir," Gillie said.

"Listen, I don't care a rat's rear end what religion y'all are," Harlow growled. "I want you at services Sunday."

"Respectfully, sir, it's against regs to demand attendance at religious services if none are offered in a soldier's chosen faith."

"I don't give a shit about regs, Sergeant," Harlow said.

"Be that as it may, Captain," Gillie said. "Regs are regs."

Harlow stood there for a long moment, glowering.

Then he turned on his heel and left our barracks.

After a silence, Tiller muttered, "I'm not a Rosicrucian. I don't even know what that is."

Gillie turned back to us. She looked pretty nonchalant for an NCO who had just defied her Captain. "Anyone in Disco Biscuit Squad is free to go to services on Sunday. Or not. As you choose."

With that, she turned and walked out of the tent.

Rosa spoke to Tiller. "I used to want to be a Rosicrucian, Tiller," she said. "If you find a service, I'll go with you."

Tiller's face reddened like he was embarrassed. He lay down on his side and turned his face away.

Miri nudged Rosa. "I think he likes you," she whispered.

"Maybe you can have a Rosicrucian wedding," Lenny suggested.

I turned to Gunner. "Are you really a *Wotansvolk?*" I asked.

Wotansvolk is a White supremacist, occult, Nazi-inspired, White revolution, neo-Pagan belief system. It's become a lot more popular and widespread in the last few years than I'd like.

"What's it to you?" Gunner asked, defiantly.

"Same thing me being a Jew is to you, Gunner," I said. "A big fat nothingburger."

"You call White genocide a nothingburger?"

"I call *you* a nothingburger, Gunner."

Gunner took a step toward me, but Sully put a restraining hand on his shoulder.

"Leave it," Sully said. "At least he didn't call you a Rosicrucian."

July 11

Today, we saw action for the first time.

I'm not sure how I feel about the term "action."

On the one hand, it certainly does involve a lot more action than the tedium of daily life at a forward operating base.

On the other hand, it makes it feel like it's supposed to be an action movie or something, which it is not – it's a *lot* less fun and satisfying.

It started as I was on my way to perimeter patrol duty. I was waylaid by Lieutenant Eggert, who asked "why is your shirt unbuttoned and untucked, soldier?"

I was confused. "Sir?" I replied. Eggert was not even my lieutenant, after all.

"Do you think you're at a rave, soldier?"

"Sir, no sir, but if you're offering, I would like to attend Jewess-palooza," I said.

"Is that a joke, soldier?"

"Sir, no sir," I said. "I really would like to attend Jewess-palooza. So would some of my friends if that can be arranged."

"Are you a funny guy, soldier?"

"Sir, no sir."

"Are you under the impression that the armed forces of the Sovereign Republic of North America are suffering from a dearth of humor in the ranks?"

"Well, now that you mention it, sir," I said. "A little bit of levity from time to time wouldn't hurt."

"Are you under the impression that war is a laughing matter, soldier?"

"Sir, no sir, I was just thinking that a laugh now and then might boost morale."

"Are you saying there's something wrong with the morale on this base?"

"Sir, yes sir," I said. "It's not great."

"Are you telling me how to run my base, soldier?"

"Is this *your* base, Lieutenant?"

"Never you mind about that," Eggert said.

"I was just thinking a little entertaining diversion might improve matters, that's all, sir."

"Were you under the impression that the military pays you to think, soldier?"

I guessed that the answer he was looking for was "no."

"Sir, no sir," I said.

"What does the military pay you for, soldier?"

It was a good question.

"To fight and die, sir?" I offered, tentatively.

"To follow orders, soldier!"

"Sir, yes sir that was going to be my next guess," I said.

"Button your shirt and tuck it in, soldier," Eggert demanded. "That's an order."

I buttoned my shirt and tucked it in, as commanded.

"Top button," he said.

"Sir?" I asked.

"Button the top button," he said.

"I have a rather thick neck, sir," I protested.

"Did I ask you for your measurements, soldier?"

"Sir, no sir," I said, "but it would have been nice if the guy who issued me my uniform had." I buttoned my top button, feeling it choke me.

Eggert scanned me up and down, skeptically.

"Dismissed," he said.

I saluted. "Sir, yes sir!" I exclaimed, just as I heard a distant series of booms followed by a whistling overhead.

Eggert looked up, annoyed.

A massive explosion blasted earth into the sky and threw me off my feet and backwards about ten feet.

I landed hard on my back and skidded in the dirt,

digging a shallow ditch in the soft ground until I came to a stop.

The concussion had knocked the breath out of me. I'd read about explosions shredding people's lungs, and I panicked for a moment as I gasped, trying to force air into my chest and find out if my respiratory system was still intact.

I felt like I'd been punched in my face by a huge fist that had also punched my entire body. My ears were ringing. I was momentarily deafened. I could not hear the distant booms, the whistling overhead, or the explosions on the ground.

But I could *see* them. Great flashes of light, cascades of earth shooting into the sky, coming down in a deluge of dirt.

All around the base.

I looked for Eggert. All I could see of him was his boots, upright, as if he'd been blown right out of them.

I wondered where he was, and if he was badly injured.

I got my answers a moment later when a torrent of meat and blood showered down on me.

I couldn't say for sure it was Eggert.

It looked like chopped sirloin. It could have *been* chopped sirloin. Maybe one of the explosives had hit the mess tent.

Except they didn't serve chopped sirloin in the mess. They served creamed chipped beef – which is not kosher, by the way but none of us Gefilte Grunts are particularly strict about keeping kosher.

I don't even know where they got the creamed chipped beef. It used to be standard fare in military mess halls decades ago. I guess it still is. Or at least it is in ours.

In any event, this stuff raining down from the sky definitely wasn't creamed chipped beef.

So, it might have been a person.

That didn't mean it was Eggert, necessarily.

But the absence of his body and presence of just his boots indicated that maybe it was.

I finally managed to gulp air into my lungs, which I guessed meant I wasn't dying, and I decided to try to stay that way.

I got to my feet and ran for the perimeter, less out of a desire to defend the base, and more out of a vague sense that the sandbags that surrounded Camp 44 might provide better protection from shrapnel than anywhere else nearby.

As I ran, explosions burst all around. My hearing suddenly returned, and the flash and shock of the detonations were now accompanied by the sound of them as well.

And by the yelling and panic and commands and sometimes the screaming of people.

I preferred the silent version.

I ran and people ran all around me, in all different directions, some with purpose, others without.

I made it to the perimeter and saw an unmanned Browning fifty caliber machine gun surrounded by sandbags. I threw myself into the enclosure of sandbags and lay on my back, hearing the explosions and feeling them convulse the world around me.

I would have preferred to remain on my back out of sight in the nest of sandbags, but two things happened:

The first was a gnawing sense of guilt that I had a duty to man that unmanned fifty cal. I read somewhere that many people who perform heroically during battle do so because they are more afraid of looking shameful in the eyes of their comrades than they are of dying.

The second thing was it occurred to me that if this bombardment was prelude to a ground attack, I'd better do my part to try to prevent it, or the sandbags wouldn't be much help if a Nazarene breached the perimeter and stabbed me in the belly with a bayonet.

Finally, I thought of Miri and Lenny and Rosa and Deb and Richie, and I realized if I had the opportunity to try to prevent a perimeter breach that could lead to their deaths, I should take it.

So, I got to my feet and manned the fifty cal.

These Brownings were among the few actual military, as opposed to civilian, weapons we had at the base, and they were powerful and fierce. I'd been trained for about five minutes on the thing, but I managed to remember how to use it, more or less.

I could see the enemy troops coming over the hill in the field beyond us. I vaguely remembered something about the range of the fifty cal – about 1800 meters.

I had no idea how to determine distance without technological assistance, but I guesstimated. I aimed and waited.

I could hear bullets flying by me. They say you don't hear the one that gets you, but I sure heard a ton that missed me. They say that's a good thing. I guess it's better than getting struck down by the one that gets you and you don't hear, but it's no day at the races, or night at the opera, or however you want to put it, because it is absolutely terrifying.

When I thought the enemy was close enough – little black dots turning into little gray army people on a canvas of grass and weeds – I began firing.

And the people I was shooting at began to fall.

So now I know what 1800 meters looks like on a battlefield.

And I know what it's like to kill somebody for the first time, from 1800 meters.

I mean, it's not like killing people is actually normal behavior. It's actually pretty aberrant behavior, and not something people should be doing under most circumstances. This is not the Wild West – or at least, it wasn't until recently. I guess it makes sense that at the age of eighteen I hadn't killed anybody. Yet.

Until today.

I mean, I can't say for certain I killed the people who fell after I fired.

But I think I did.

I'm pretty certain, actually.

The big chunks of them that went flying off their bodies were a pretty clear giveaway. I could see that even from the distance between us, and I'm pretty sure most people die when that happens. They say a fifty cal can take a chunk out of a person the size of a grapefruit. I can't pretend I measured it that closely as I fired, but it certainly looked like I was doing substantial damage to the bodies of human beings 1800 feet or less from me.

It took me two tries before most of the people I was shooting at began to fall as chunks of them went flying. The Browning fifty cal has a tremendous kick, and it rattles your body and brain, and it took a moment or two until I could figure out how to hold it steady and aim true.

But once I figured it out, I got pretty good at it.

I'm not proud of that.

But I prefer it to the alternative.

So, this went on for a while.

I fired. They fired. I heard bullets whiz past my ears. I heard bullets thud into the sandbags surrounding me.

I continued to fire. The enemy continued to fall. Chunks of them went flying off their bodies. Shells continued to whistle overhead. Explosions continued to rock the camp and blast craters in the ground. Between the Browning's recoil and the shells hitting the ground, I was in a constant state of violent vibration.

I wasn't alone, of course. Machine gun nests dotted the perimeter of our camp, and we were all firing at the enemy as they skulked towards us. We had pretty good coverage of the field of battle. There was nowhere a Nazarene could advance without facing the fire from our Brownings.

I figured it was only a matter of time before something – a bullet, an explosion, an enemy soldier breaching the perimeter – got me. I was hoping the enemy would give up before that happened.

I was hoping we wouldn't be the ones to surrender, because I didn't know if the Nazarenes were into taking prisoners, or what they did with them when they took them.

Especially the Jewish ones.

So, I kept firing, they kept falling, and more of them kept coming over the hill. With every wave, they inched closer and closer to the wire.

Then a series of detonations burst behind the hills, fire mushrooming upwards into the sky, and the shells stopped falling on Camp 44.

I was confused, although I didn't have time to be *too* confused. I knew we didn't have an air force. So where did the explosions come from that had taken out the Nazarene's batteries?

In any case, the Nazarene infantry was till creeping towards us, gaining ground slowly and painfully and at great human cost, but gaining, nonetheless. So, I kept firing, hoping to contribute to them gaining a little less, or maybe stop gaining altogether.

Then the advancing enemy disappeared in a surge of flame. The field between the camp and the hills was blasted into the sky, along with the enemy soldiers. I could feel the heat of the explosions on my face, and the concussion knocked me back off my feet.

When the smoke cleared, the field was nothing but charred corpses and upturned dirt, along with pockets of fire still burning. Another round of explosions detonated behind the hills and then into the forest beyond, setting the trees ablaze.

The battle was over. I wasn't sure what was supposed to come next, but I didn't care. I slung my Savage semi-auto rifle over my shoulder, left my post, and headed back to Disco Biscuit Squad's tent.

On the way, I ran into Captain Harlow.

"Why is your collar unbuttoned, soldier?" he demanded.

I reached for my throat and realized that my collar was, indeed, unbuttoned. I had no memory of having unbuttoned it during the battle.

"The rattle of my Browning fifty caliber must have shaken it loose, sir," I said, and turned and walked away from him as quickly as possible. My ears were still ringing, so I ignored the words he shouted at my back. I was afraid if I responded, I'd march right back to him and punch him in the throat.

I did a quick cost benefit analysis and decided the gain would not justify the pain.

I ran into Miri on my way back to our tent. Like me, she was hot and sweaty and dirty, and had a look on her face like what had just happened would haunt her forever.

I was so freaking happy to find her alive.

I guess she felt the same way, because without discussing it, we snuck behind a storage container and had the quickest quickie -- and also the best -- that I could have ever imagined.

If I were a poet, I might say that having seen death and faced death, we wanted to affirm life through the union of our bodies.

But if I'm honest, I think it's closer to the truth to say that after our first firefight, we were both desperate for something that would make us feel less shitty.

July 12

When today began, I was still hopeful we might be given leave to attend Jewess-palooza, which began today.

Be careful what you wish for.

At breakfast, we learned that the explosions that had won the battle for us were made by drones. Apparently, the Sovereign Republic has drones – a lot of them -- if not a proper air force.

That gives us a tactical advantage.

I was glad to hear it.

I'll take any kind of advantage we can get.

Late morning, news began to break that the Jewess-palooza festival, which was being held in the Jefferson County Fairgrounds in nearby Hillsboro, was under attack.

Information was sketchy, but it involved Nazarene troops in uniform riding pick-up trucks, motorcycles, and paragliders, and carrying automatic weapons.

As soon as Gillie heard the news, she ordered us to gear up. But when we went to the motor pool to commandeer some vehicles, we were met by Captain Harlow, who gave us the stern face.

"Stand down, Sergeant," he said.

"No can do, sir," Gillie responded.

"We have not been authorized to intervene," Harlow said.

"All due respect, sir, Disco Biscuit is intervening."

"Stand down, Gilroy."

"We're the closest operating base to the fairgrounds, sir."

"I'm not making a request, Sergeant. I'm giving you an order."

Gillie took a deep breath and let it out, slowly.

"Captain, over a third of my squad are Gefilte Grunts. No way are they gonna sit this one out."

"It's not up for negotiation, Sergeant."

"Captain, it should be all hands-on deck to meet this attack. All I'm asking you for is one squad. One. Don't try to hold us back, sir. You can have me court martialed for insubordination, but you're not stopping me from taking my squad to try to put down this thing. Those are kids at a music festival. We're going, authorization or not. If you want to waste a good NCO like me by jamming me up with a court martial, have at it. But you'll have to wait until we get back."

"I can have the MPs here in a second," Captain Harlow said.

"I'll be out of here in half that time," Gillie said.

The captain screwed up his face and growled in his throat.

"Don't expect any reinforcements, Gilroy," he said. "You get yourselves in a fix, you're on your own."

"Copy that, Captain," Gillie said. She turned back to us. "Saddle up, Disco Biscuits. Cavalry is on the way."

When Disco Biscuit Squad arrived forty-five minutes later outside Jewess-palooza, riding Jeeps instead of horses or even Hum Vees, we found New Confederacy Nazarene soldiers firing into civilian vehicles trying to flee the fairgrounds.

This was the first time I had seen the enemy up close. The Nazarenes were dressed in what looked like modified old Confederacy uniforms – grey with a high collar and a gray cap with a black visor. I assumed they were made of cotton rather than the wool from which the originals were made.

Or maybe they'd been raided from a Halloween costume store.

The Nazarenes were shouting "*Judenrät!* Praise

Jesus!" and "May thousands die in the name of the Christian National Crusade! May thousands die in the name of Christian National Resistance!"

"*Judenrät*" is actually German for "Jewish Council," which were the governing bodies the Nazis set up to allow Jewish ghettos to – supposedly – govern themselves. It was an odd choice of terminology, but I don't think the Nazarenes really knew what it meant.

As we pulled up to the stopped cars and the Nazarene gunmen shooting through the windows I jumped out and fired at the nearest Confederate. The blast from my Savage punched through his skull and out the other side.

That was the first time I'd killed anyone up close.

By the time the day was done, it would prove not to be the last.

Killing someone up close is different than doing the same from far away.

But I didn't really have time to think about that.

We continued on foot. The Nazarenes were so intent on their purpose that they did not at first even notice us. I fired several quick shots, taking down half a dozen of them, one after the other. My squad mates did likewise.

The Nazarenes realized they were being fired upon, and they haphazardly returned fire as they retreated back into the fairgrounds upon which the festival had been held.

Why hadn't the festival been cancelled, I wondered, after yesterday's attack? My guess was that the authorities thought the Jefferson County Fairgrounds were far enough from the front to proceed.

They also probably thought the fighting was over, and we had won.

They also probably thought if the enemy were going to run through our lines, they would have picked a target with more strategic importance than a bunch of kids at a music festival.

I mean, why wouldn't they think that? I thought the

same thing.

What no one had yet figured out was just how irrationally and completely the New Christian Confederacy of the Nazarene Nation really, really, really hated Jews.

After today, though, I think everyone will be pretty clear on that.

We entered the festival grounds, and I saw a white van, and a woman lying beside it, her hands on her belly. I went to her, while the rest of the squad fanned out.

The woman was alive but had been shot in the abdomen. She was moaning in pain. I looked inside the van and found a man lying on his back with his eyes wide open. His shirt was covered in blood. I checked for a pulse.

"Is my husband Ok?" the woman on the ground asked me.

"He should make it," I lied.

Her husband was dead.

I heard the screech of car brakes and turned around to see a pick-up truck pull up and about a half dozen Nazarenes pile out of the truck bed.

I grabbed the injured woman by her collar and dragged her around to the far side of the van, firing at the Nazarenes as I went. She cried in pain as I dragged her.

I laid her down with the wheel well for protection, and then I went to the other wheel well and began firing over the hood of the van.

I hit one Nazarene as he was taking aim at me. Another fired an RPG. The RPG sailed over the van. I heard it explode somewhere behind me and felt the force and heat of the concussion slam into my back.

The guy with the RPG reloaded, but I managed to put him down before he fired. The RPG sailed into his own pick-up truck, and the resulting explosion killed all but two of the remaining Nazarenes.

I took aim at the surviving two, but then a fusillade of

semi-automatic weapon fire erupted to my right, and I saw Gillie and Gunner heading towards us, firing at the Nazarenes.

I never thought I'd be glad to see Gunner until that moment.

The two remaining Nazarenes went down, and then I saw something in the sky.

"Look," I called out, pointing up.

Gillie and Gunner turned to look.

Two dozen Nazarenes on paragliders were sailing over the stadium walls and heading towards us.

They looked sort of like condors, weirdly peaceful soaring there in the sky, wings framed against eggshell blue and white cotton clouds.

Then they started firing their weapons at us.

"Shit," Gunner said, raising his rifle and firing.

We took out at least six of them, but then two more pick-ups pulled up and at least a dozen Nazarenes piled out, weapons raised, yelling at us to surrender.

Sensing the three of us couldn't shoot our way out, Gillie laid her rifle on the ground and raised her hands in surrender. Gunner and I did likewise. Meanwhile Nazarenes on paragliders were landing inside the stadium and heading out to search for more victims.

"Where are your Jews?" a Nazarene sergeant asked.

"I'm sorry, what?" Gillie said.

"Tell your Jewish soldiers to step forward," the sergeant said. "They'll get a chance to convert."

"A battlefield conversion?" Gillie asked.

"If they want to live," the sergeant said.

"We don't have any Jews," Gillie said. "And we are all Jews."

The sergeant looked at her, perplexed.

Then he raised his rifle, the barrel pointed to her forehead.

I glanced at Gunner. I was afraid he was going to give

me away.

Gunner glanced at me. "You think Jews are worth dying for?" he muttered.

He was telling me not to let Gillie die to protect me.

I stepped forward. "I'm a Jew," I said.

The sergeant lowered his rifle. He fished in his pocket and pulled out a mini bible. He held it toward me.

"On your knees," he said.

"I'm good here," I said.

"On your knees, kiss the book, and declare your soul unto Jesus," he said.

"No, thanks," I said. "I'm good."

The sergeant pulled his sidearm with his free hand, thumbed back the hammer, and pointed it at me.

"If you do as I say, you'll be taken prisoner and treated in accordance with the Geneva convention," he said. "If you don't, your blood can fertilize the soil you're standing on right now."

"You don't call it 'Blood and Soil' for nothing, I guess," I said. I knew I was playing with my life, but I figured I was probably dead, anyway, no matter what I did or said.

"Make your choice," the sergeant said.

"I'll take option number three," I said.

"There is no option number three," the sergeant said.

"There's always an option number three," I said, although I didn't believe it for a second.

A shot rang out, and the sergeant's head snapped back in a misty spray of blood and brain, and he went down.

Turns out, there actually *was* an option number three.

We hit the dirt as we saw Lenny, Rosa, Miri, Deb, Richie, and two others I didn't know heading towards the Nazarenes, firing their weapons in unison.

The two strangers were in the same tan work-clothes from Wal Mart with stripes stitched on the sleeves that we wore. So, they were Sovereign Republic soldiers. They were a man and a woman. They were both olive-skinned. The woman wore a headscarf.

The Nazarenes started to go down. Gillie and Gunner and I retrieved our weapons and joined the firefight.

We were still outnumbered, but we managed to put down the Nazarenes in about five minutes. I think the New Confederates, for all their belligerence, were disadvantaged by their zeal for pogroms and battlefield religious conversions, which gave an edge to those of us focused on combat instead of slaughtering civilian music festival attendees.

"This is Omar and Fatima," Lenny said, introducing us to the newcomers, after we had put down the last of this group of Nazarenes. "They're siblings from Michigan. Their squad is called the Dearborn Arabian Knights."

"We didn't choose the name," Fatima said, as she knelt down beside the woman with the belly wound, who was moaning weakly, and began to administer first aid. She carried a small medical kit at her side. In this war, it seemed, the medics had to shoot first and heal later.

"They know we're Jews," Lenny added.

"They're Ok with it," Rosa added.

"As long as you're not Nazarenes," Omar said. "We're good."

With more reinforcements from Dearborn, we quickly spread out and in about an hour, we had taken the fairgrounds. Most of the Nazarenes died fighting. We took about a dozen prisoners.

We found bodies of concert goers hacked to pieces by machetes.

We found a storage room where people had gone to hide, and the Nazarenes had tossed in grenades and killed them all.

We found the bodies of couples bound together with wire and set on fire.

We found young women and teenage girls with their

clothes ripped off their bodies.

A forensic team would be needed to know for sure, but it sure looked like they had been raped before they had been killed.

What had started as a celebration of Jewish music and Jewish women had had been targeted for exactly that reason.

"I don't know if we're going to win this war with our neighbors to the south," Miri said, "But it's pretty clear that we can't afford to lose."

July 13

The body count at the festival was estimated at 1200, with two hundred and forty hostages believed to have been kidnapped, possibly to be offered as wives to the most impressively holy warriors of the Nazarene Christian Crusaders, which is what they called their soldiers.

After chow, Gillie gathered the squad for a briefing.

"Please be advised that if your dog tags read anything other than 'P' for your religious designation, it is recommended that you destroy them if you are in immediate danger of being taken prisoner," she informed us. "Word is that the Nazarenes are checking dog tags and forcing what they call 'battlefield conversions' on non-protestant POWs. Those who do not comply are summarily executed. This violates the Geneva convention, but they don't seem super-concerned about that, since their Christian Nation, or whatever they call it, is the only earthly authority they respect. Let me say something else here. There are reports coming from southern Kentucky that some of our soldiers turned over their Jewish, Muslim, and Catholic fellow citizens to the Nazarenes when captured. I'm going to be as clear as I can about this. That's not going to happen in Disco Biscuit Squad. We are not going to turn on our own. Anyone thinks they can't abide by that, you come speak to me. I'll have you transferred to another squad, no questions asked. But if you stay with Disco Biscuit and you rat out one of our team, I will make it my business to see you pay for that treachery, one way or the other – even if that means putting a bullet in your head myself. 'Are Jews worth dying for?' I heard someone ask that question at the music festival yesterday. Here's the answer. Your squad is worth dying for. Every goddamn one of them, Jewish or otherwise. Don't you forget it."

Later, Lenny, Miri, Rosa, and I huddled together by the latrines.

"Do you think we can trust our squad not to turn us in?" Lenny asked.

"I think Gillie really would kill them if they did," Miri said.

"But what if Gillie is killed in action and the enemy captures the squad?" Lenny asked.

"We've got a Catholic, a Hindu, a Rastafarian," Rosa said. "They'd all be thrown under the bus if someone ratted us out. Who would do that?"

We all looked at each other and we all knew the answer.

"Gunner might," Miri said.

"Gunner might rat out everyone who doesn't have a 'P' on their dog tags," Lenny said.

"But he didn't rat me out at the fairgrounds," I said.

"Yeah," Lenny said. "But Gillie was right there."

"Something he might not do in front of Gillie," Rosa said, "he might do somewhere else."

We were silent for a few moments, thinking it over.

"Should we frag him?" Lenny asked.

I looked at him sharply. "You've been watching too many Vietnam movies," I said.

"We could do it," Lenny said. "Next time we're in a firefight, or there's an attack on the camp. One stray bullet would do the trick, and no one would even think to ask any questions."

It was a sound plan, but I hated it.

Miri, it turned out, hated it even more. "No," she said. "We're not doing that."

"You wouldn't have to do it," Lenny said. "I'd do it."

"That's not who we are," Miri said.

"That's not who *you* are," Lenny said. "I'm an entirely different proposition."

"It's not who you are either, Lenny," Miri said.

"I'm flattered by your faith in my character, Miri," Lenny said. "But that's *exactly* who I am."

"You've never done anything like that in your life, Len," I said.

"Everybody's got to start somewhere," Lenny said.

"It's not who you deserve to be," Miri insisted. "It's not who your brothers and sisters *deserve you* to be. It's not who your cousin Rosa deserves you to be. And it's not who your future sister-in-law deserves you to be."

Lenny looked at Miri like he was surprised that someone would care so much about what kind of person he was or should be.

"What if he tries to rat us out, though?" Lenny asked.

"Then you can do whatever you want to him," Miri said. "But not until then."

"But by then it might be too late," Lenny said.

"That's a risk we'll have to take," Miri said, firmly.

Lenny nodded, thoughtfully. "Ok, sis," he said. "You deserve to have a brother-in-law you're not ashamed of. I'll try to be that brother-in-law for you."

Miri went to him and embraced him.

It wasn't a casually friendly or merely sisterly hug.

It was a very serious hug. A *thank G-d you chose not to take that turn into total dick-itude for the rest of your life* hug.

And Lenny hugged her back.

And, in a way, I think he was grateful.

He would have willingly sacrificed his soul for the safety of his family and friends.

But I think he appreciated having a compelling reason not to.

The End

Peter Ullian is the author of the Science Fiction & Fantasy Poetry Association's Rhysling Award-nominated poem "Nixon's Planet," subsequently included in the SFPA's 2019 anthology. He is also the author of the short story "The Vietnamization of Centauri V," published in the DAW Books anthology *Star Colonies*. His Amazon Short, "To Repair the World," received over 200 five-star reader reviews. Peter is also the author of the short stories "The Sun Sets on the Hall of Justice," published in the anthology *Crimeucopia -- Say What Now?* from Murderous Ink Press; "Ribbons and Tin" and "Owen's Blood," both published in *Cemetery Dance Magazine*; and "The Ballad of Beeve Wellington," "Apprehending Mr. Howard," and "Dreaming of Pesach with the Last Bandito," all published in *Frontier Tales Magazine*. His post-apocalypse Cli-Fi novel, *The Last Electric House*, is published by Swamp Angel Press.

Peter has written screenplays for major and independent film studios, such as Paramount, Hollywood Pictures, and Zeal Pictures. Peter also served as the 2019-2020 Poet Laureate of Beacon, New York. His poetry is published in anthologies and periodicals; in the chapbook *Secret Histories and Exobiologies* from Poet's Haven; and in the full-length anthology *The Fevered Dream-Crimes of Pulp Fiction Poets and Other Love Stories* from Autumn Lion Music Publishing. His poetry has been nominated for the Pushcart Prize.

Additionally, Peter's work for the stage has been produced off-Broadway, regionally, and internationally, and directed by such major theatre artists as Harold Prince, David Esbjornson, and Lynne Taylor-Corbett. Publications of his plays include *Big Bossman* and *The Triumphant Return of Blackbird* Flynt (Broadway Play Publishing), *New American Century & Fair City* and *Pan-American* (NoPassport Press), and *Valhalla Correctional,* included in the anthology *When the Promise Was Broken: Short Plays Inspired by the Songs of Bruce Springsteen* (Smith & Krauss). His other theatrical work includes *Flight of the Lawnchair Man, Eliot Ness in Cleveland, Hester Street Hideaway – a Lower East Side Love Story,* and *Signs of Life.* He has received numerous awards for his dramatic writing including the Roger L Stevens Award from the Kennedy Center/Fund for New American Plays and production grants from the National Endowment for the Arts and the New York Foundation for the Arts.